Persuading Miss Mary

Persuading Miss Mary

A Pride and Prejudice Variation

LEENIE BROWN

LEENIE B BOOKS
HALIFAX

Cover design by Leenie B Books. Images sourced from Deposit Photos and Period Images.

Persuading Miss Mary © 2019 Leenie Brown. All Rights Reserved, except where otherwise noted.

ISBN (print) 978-1-989410-40-0; (ebooks) 978-1-989410-41-7(mobi), 978-1-989410-42-4(epub)

Contents

Dear Reader,

Once upon a time...well, actually, a few years ago, I began a weekly writing exercise on my blog (leeniebrown.com) and called it Thursday's Three Hundred. What was supposed to be just a few minutes of practice – just three hundred words a week – quickly took on a life of its own and became something much grander.

Those writing exercises have now produced several published works, including the one you hold in your hands.

While some things about how I create these stories have evolved since that first writing exercise, the tradition of posting a portion of a story continues each Thursday. In fact, there is a story posting there now.

Chapter 1

"What do you mean I am not allowed entrance?" Reginald Fitzwilliam, Viscount Westonbury, glared at Mr. Nibley, Matlock House's longtime butler.

"Just that, my lord. The countess has informed me that you are not allowed entrance without specific invitation."

"But it is my home!"

Mr. Nibley did not flinch. "Not at present, my lord. Your residence is the house in Brook Street."

"The house in Brook Street?" Wes huffed and looked at the sky above him before continuing. "I fully realize that my residence is in Brook Street. However, this is also my home, and I will not leave without seeing my mother."

Mr. Nibley paused for a moment as if considering whether or not he should disturb his mistress.

Wes waved toward the house. "My mother, if you will."

"I shall see if she is home to callers."

"I am not a caller! I am her son!"

"Yes, my lord." Finally, the staid man before Wes shifted uneasily. "I only do as I am told, my lord."

Wes clenched his jaw and shook his head. "Am I allowed to wait inside while you check?"

Mr. Nibley gave a slight shake of his head. "I do apologize, my lord, but I have my orders."

"Oh, for the love of –," he stopped when Mr. Nibley coughed. "Yes, yes, I know. Mother cannot abide such language, and I promise to not resort to such as long as my mother sees me. If she will not, then I shall be forced to vent my spleen with whatever colourful language I choose and at whatever volume I wish to shout it."

The butler gave a nod of his head and hurried into Matlock House to see if his mistress was willing to see her eldest son, who was left to mutter oaths under his breath on the step and wonder what bee had flown into his mother's bonnet. She had not locked him out of the house in years!

The last time had been when a gentleman had shown up to collect a debt from Lord Matlock which had been incurred by his son, who should have been at school and not in some gambling hell. Being locked out of the house, coupled with the removal of his allowance until the sum had been repaid fully and half again, had worked well. Westonbury never set foot in a gambling hell after that, and his bills were always paid before word of any outstanding sums reached the ears of his mother.

For most gentlemen, their fathers were to be feared, and Lord Matlock was no exception. However, Lady Matlock was a good bit more fearsome to her sons than their father for she was cunning in her punishments, which were always doled out as if they were the most natural things in the world. If one took a step off a cliff, one must experience a fall. That was his mother's philosophy. Therefore, if you stole a biscuit, you spent the day in the kitchen assisting the scullery maid.

She loved her sons fiercely. Too fiercely at times, if you asked Lord Westonbury. He shook his head and chuckled. His mother had an uncanny ability to anticipate how he might attempt to escape a punishment or to find a bit of fun. She had been sitting below his window on more than one occasion at their estate when, as a young boy, he had been required to stay indoors for some indiscretion such as tormenting the stable cats.

The door opened interrupting Wes's contemplation of his mother.

"My lady will see you in the green sitting room, and only in the green sitting room."

Just as he suspected, she expected him to decide on where they would meet, which he had been considering. His mother was not fond of the small drawing room off of the library, and that would have been precisely where he would have told Nibley that his mother could meet him. But again, she had thwarted his enjoyment by anticipating his move.

He handed his hat and walking stick to Mr. Nibley before removing his great coat.

"Am I allowed to direct myself to said room, or must I wait to be announced?"

The right corner of Mr. Nibley's mouth tipped upward but only just. "Do you wish to be announced, my lord?"

Wes chuckled. Mr. Nibley might appear to be wholly stoic, but he was not immune to the desire to have a bit of fun on occasion. "Indeed, I think I must be if I am merely a caller. Do you remember my name?"

"The name you use at every house, my lord?"

"No, the one that is precisely designed to annoy my mother."

"I think I do."

"Then, lead on my good man, and I shall not turn you out when I become master of Matlock House."

"I am sure I will not even be alive when that happens, my lord."

"I do hope that is not true. Not that I am wishing for my father's demise, of course."

"I did not think you were, my lord." Mr. Nibley began leading Wes down the hall to the green sitting room. The only sitting room on the ground floor — the room which was designated for calls and not much else.

The upper servant stepped into the room and, in a voice he might use if he were speaking to someone at the other end of a grand ballroom filled with dancers awaiting the start of the music, said "My lord, Reginald Arthur Fitzwilliam, Viscount Westonbury, the first-born and heir of the body of Lord Matlock, long may he live, to see Lady Matlock."

"Nibley," Lady Matlock scolded.

"I am only doing my duty, my lady," the butler replied with a bow before ducking out of the room.

"If he were not put up to such a thing by you, I would see him reprimanded properly."

"No, you would not," Wes said as he took a chair near where his mother was perched on her favourite sofa with a dog next to her. "Is that not Darcy's beast?"

"Beast? Dash is not a beast, are you, boy?" His mother scratched Dash's ear. "He is here to keep your brother company while he recovers."

"Then why is he here rather than with Richard?"

"Why are you here?"

Wes raised an eyebrow at his mother's coy response. "Because this is the only room in which I was allowed." He crossed his arms and leveled a disdainful look in Lady Matlock's direction. "Would you care to explain to me what I have done that has resulted in my exile from my home?"

"You are banned from the house in Brook Street?"

"Mother."

She chuckled and shrugged. "Impertinence is rather bothersome; is it not?"

"Yes, Mother. Now, if you would answer me seriously."

"I have guests."

"That is no reason for me to be stopped at the door to my home."

She shrugged again. "It is if the father of one of my guests has expressed concern regarding you."

Wes's brow furrowed. Who was visiting his mother?

"And, since the arrival of my guests, I have heard a most disturbing story from one of them."

"I still do not –"

"About you."

"I beg your pardon? You have heard a disturbing story about me?"

"Yes." She fluttered her lashes at him but said no more.

For a full minute, he only glared at her. It was a futile attempt to goad her into speaking, and he knew it. Still, it had to be attempted. "Oh, very well, what have I done?"

"I understand Miss Lydia and her sister met you in London." She lifted her chin slightly. "Quite often the ladies at such places as where you met them have been tossed out of their homes."

His waiting on the front step was beginning to make sense.

"Now, I know that there are gentlemen who frequent such places." She watched her hand stroke Dash's fur rather than looking at him. A faint pink tinged her cheeks. "However, they are not where I would wish my son to –"

"Please, Mother. I understand your meaning." He was likely as uncomfortable with this topic of conversation as she was. "However, I believe I am old enough to make my own decisions about such things."

She sighed. "Of course, you are." Her voice was just above a whisper and laced with disappointment. She lifted her eyes to him. "I only wished to make my point."

"I shall consider what you have said."

"Thank you."

"Am I reinstated as someone who can visit without an invitation?"

She shook her head. "I fear not. As long as Miss Lydia and Miss Bennet are staying here, you must be a stranger."

Wes blinked. "Miss Lydia and Miss Bennet are here?" Miss Mary Bennet was here at his parents' home? Walking the halls he had walked all his life? Sleeping in one of their guest rooms?

"Yes, I thought it good to have an ally in seeing that Richard recovers as he should, and, since Miss Kitty is visiting Georgiana, Miss Mary was sent to keep her sister company. However, there is not a lot of love lost between you and Miss Mary, so her father was concerned that being in a place where you might meet regularly might provoke her into besmirching the Bennet name. You know how it is. If someone should be calling and hear a young lady speaking plainly to a gentleman, the young lady will be the one taken to task."

"I would not provoke her."

His mother's replying look told him that she did not believe such a thing was possible, and truth be told, it likely was not. Miss Mary did not treat him as anyone else did – save for his closest family members and best friend. To her, he was merely a gentleman – not a viscount or the future Earl of Matlock. And confound it all if it was not refreshing!

"Then, am I only allowed to call during proper hours and in only this room, or will I be allowed to visit my brother?"

His mother sighed. "Your father will say you are welcome to visit your brother and join us for dinner and all those such things. However, neither he nor I will tolerate any provocation of our guests."

Wes nodded.

"I like her."

Wes's brow furrowed. "Miss Lydia?"

"Yes, her, but also her sister. Miss Mary is no wilting wallflower. I quite approve of that even if she does need a little softening."

Her head tilted to the side as she looked at him. So, this was her true purpose. She saw Miss Mary as a project of sorts.

"Just be kind to her," she added. "That is all I ask. Treat her as you would Georgiana."

That was a little bit impossible. He had never had a dream about Georgiana being in his bed. However, he was not about to say such to his mother. Instead, he dutifully assured her that he would do his best to behave as she expected.

"And if you could stop frequenting that place – Sally's, I believe it is called."

"Mother."

"I just think it would help you improve in the eyes of Miss Mary."

"I said I would consider what you had said. I will not promise any further."

She sighed. "I suppose I will have to be satisfied with that."

"Yes, you will. Now, am I allowed to see my brother?"

Lady Matlock glanced at the clock before rising. "Yes, I do believe he will be rising and making his way to the library."

"Rising? Do not tell me he is still taking a rest each afternoon." He rose to follow her from the room, but Dash stepped between Wes and his mother.

"He most certainly is. But it is not my doing." She smiled over her shoulder at him.

"Miss Lydia?"

She nodded. "As I said, I wanted to have an ally in seeing Richard recover."

Wes laughed as he followed his mother and Dash up the stairs. "Have I complimented you lately on your deviousness?"

"No, I do not believe you have," she replied with a chuckle. "There is a soiree that you must attend the day after next."

"Mother."

"You must marry someday, Reginald. The nursery has been empty for far too long."

"You forget, my lady," he said as he came to a stop on the landing next to her. "My residence is in Brook Street."

She patted his cheek. "Only until you marry. Then, you are free to bring my daughter and your children here to be with me."

Chapter 2

Lady Matlock stopped at the door to the library and gave Wes a pointed look. "Be polite," she whispered.

Wes rolled his eyes. He was not an infant in need of reminding how to behave. Had she not less than five minutes ago told him to be polite? The walk up the stairs and down the hall had not jogged her instructions from his mind.

"Your brother has come to see you, Richard," his mother said as she bustled into the library. Her eyes surveyed the room before coming to rest on his brother. Then, with a further pointed look in Wes's direction, she took a seat near Miss Mary who was reading near the window.

"Miss Bennet," he said with a bow. "Miss Lydia." He again bowed. "It was a pleasant surprise to hear that you are guests at Matlock House for a time.

You made no mention of it when I was in Hertfordshire last."

"That is because Mary did not wish for you to know," Lydia replied with a smirk. "Surprises are delightful. Are they not?"

Wes settled into a chair closer to his brother than to Miss Mary but not altogether too far from where she was sitting.

"Were you surprised by the arrival of the Miss Bennets?" he asked Richard. "Or am I the only one?"

His brother chuckled.

So, he was the only one not to know of the plans for the Bennets to be guests of his mother.

"I will admit to being privy to the surprise." His brother's eyes were dancing with amusement.

"I am certain a surprise such as I received would not be best for one's recovery," Wes said flatly.

The fact that everyone knew of Miss Mary and Miss Lydia's arrival, save him, grated. It was as if not a soul in this room trusted him. What did they expect him to do? Await Miss Mary in her room so that he might argue with her until she allowed him to take her to bed? His left eyebrow lifted as the idea of such a thing played itself out in his mind.

"I have already explained why you did not know about my guests," his mother said sternly.

Wes wondered for a moment before he recovered himself, after being caught woolgathering, if she had been reading his mind, for her look was as severe as her tone.

"Yes, I am not to be trusted." He attempted to keep his tone flat and not one which spoke to his great displeasure with the whole situation.

A small, quiet burst of laughter caught his ear and drew his eyes to Miss Mary, who was diligently smirking at her book. The taunting lass! What he wouldn't do at this moment to be alone with her and discover just what she was thinking.

"How is your head?" He pulled his eyes away from the way the neckline of Miss Mary's green day dress rose to her throat while a tidy line of buttons marched down from there to the sash beneath her breasts. Such a lack of exposed flesh was surprisingly enticing.

"I cannot yet read a book for any great length of time, but I find that the floor no longer meets my feet before they expect it," Richard replied.

"And the eyes?"

"Not much has changed, and it may never correct itself."

"And your commission?"

Richard grimaced. "Father is seeing what can be done about it."

Wes knew that his brother was not the sort who had ever preferred sitting by and watching anything.

"There is the estate your grandfather left for my youngest son," their mother inserted. "It is not without the potential to increase its value." She smiled at Richard. "I am not happy that you have been injured or that your eyes are not what they were, but I am excessively glad to have you home."

To Wes's surprise, his brother who lived for change and adventure agreed that he was also glad to be home. The comment was accompanied by a speaking look for Miss Lydia.

"When do you marry?"

"Reginald!"

"It is not as if it is a taboo topic," Wes protested. "Anyone with sense can see that a marriage is in the offing. It is the only feasible option for two people so obviously in love. Did you not hear Mr. Bennet or the song at Darcy's wedding?"

His mother pursed her lips. "It is not polite to ask such a thing. Your brother will share what news he has with you when he chooses to share it, and not before. Hold your tongue." Her lips tilted upward. "Not that I am not anxiously awaiting such news myself."

"It would not be wise to make any promises before I know what will become of me," Richard inserted.

"September," Lydia replied. "I think September would be a lovely time for a wedding. Or October," she added.

Her brow was furrowed as if she was thinking deeply.

"November is also a nice month, but beyond that, travel is not the best. Why last year, there were four days of dreadful rain before Mr. Bingley's ball. It was a trial, I assure you, to be forced to remain at home because the roads were in such a state. There was very little time to add any new trimmings to dresses. Do you not remember that, Mary?"

"How could one forget being trapped in her home with sisters who were in desperate want of lace and who had no gentlemen to call on them, save our cousin, Mr. Collins."

"Oh, it was horrid!" Lydia cried.

"Mr. Collins? This is the rector at Hunsford?" Lady Matlock asked.

"Does not anyone wish to know about a September wedding?" How could his mother move on from her son's lady announcing an autumn wedding without so much as an inquisitive look? "Or is this another thing which is to remain a surprise for me?"

Not a soul seemed to hear him. Miss Lydia's tales of her horrid cousin would not be stymied by his curiosity about a wedding.

"Do you think things will be settled enough for an autumn wedding?" he attempted to turn the conversation once again.

"Oh, most certainly," Lydia assured him before turning back to Lady Matlock. "And Elizabeth was put upon to promise him the first dance. She never liked him, but Mama thought it would be an excellent thing if one of her daughters were to marry him since he is the heir to Longbourn." She shrugged. "I had thought Mary would be the best choice. She reads sermons, you know."

Mary rolled her eyes. "And you read plays. Does that mean you must wed the owner of a theatre?"

"Well, I would not have minded doing so if I had met one who captured my heart."

"A theatre owner? You would have married a theatre owner if you had thought yourself in love with him?" Mary asked incredulously.

Wes smiled. Apparently, he was not the only person with whom Miss Bennet liked to argue.

"I would not have lacked for entertainment," Lydia replied. "And I might have even tried my hand at acting. I think I would be quite good at it."

"Do you know what sorts of ladies grace the stage?" Mary snapped her book closed.

"Ones which can act," Wes answered in Lydia's place. "Most are pleasant to look upon, but a few are, well, shall we just say that not every role calls for a beautiful maiden."

"I would guess most are not maidens," Mary muttered as she opened her book once again.

"I would agree," Wes whispered in her direction. His mother's brow furrowed, her lips pursed, and he feared if he left the house at this very moment, he would never again be allowed to re-enter.

"I am sure you know best about such things," Mary replied without taking her eyes off her book.

"I like plays, but I have never darkened the halls behind the stage. I prefer to see the actors and actresses from my box."

Mary shrugged one shoulder as if to say she did not believe him.

"It really does not matter," Lydia inserted before Wes could say something which would likely have his mother calling for footmen to escort him from the house. "I did not fall in love with a theatre owner. I fell in love with someone far better."

She ducked her head slightly as Richard wrapped his hand around hers, and though he could not hear it, Wes could feel the sigh that accompanied the rise and fall of his brother's shoulders. For a moment, as the room sat silent, he wondered what it must feel like to be so at peace and to know that he was so well-loved by a beautiful young woman such as Miss Lydia. Maybe one day he would discover that answer.

"We should go to the theatre," Lady Matlock said, breaking the silence. "Reginald, I shall leave it to you to make the arrangements. Do make sure it is appropriate for our guests."

"Is Richard able to join us?"

"I think I can manage such excitement."

"Oh, I should think so," Lydia agreed. "And you can always close your eyes if need be."

Wes was impressed both by the prodigious good care Miss Lydia provided for his brother and the fact that Richard allowed it. If their mother had suggested such a thing, Richard would have likely grumbled something about not being so weak as to need to close his eyes. However, since Miss Lydia had said it, it was an excellent idea. Wes shook his head. His mother was cunning. Very, very cunning.

"I will provide you with a list of soirees we must attend so that you can decide when it would be best for our trip to the theatre to take place."

"A list of soirees?" She had only mentioned one earlier. Perhaps he should have remained on the steps instead of insisting that he be allowed to see her. "Have you accepted them all on my behalf?"

She fluttered her lashes at him. "Why, of course, I did. We ladies will need someone to escort us."

"Cannot Father do that?" He could feel her circling, drawing in her regiment of logic, waiting to snare him.

"Your father rarely dances. He spends most of his time discussing politics and pretending to play cards."

"Will Miss Lydia even wish to attend soirees without Richard?"

"That is a good question, but not one we have not already considered. Lydia must be introduced to society, and Richard will attend what he can when he feels he can. However, if he needs to return home before an event is over, he is to leave, in which case, your carriage would be most welcome. Small steps must be taken to see what can and cannot be tolerated. Therefore, we are beginning with a musicale the day after next. I have heard that the Johnsons will be there. Their daughter is a very pretty young lady."

Richard chuckled.

"Were you not pushing her at Richard at one time?" Wes shook his head.

"I was, but Richard has found himself a lady."

Wes braced himself for what he knew were going to be her next words.

"I promise to stop pushing eligible young ladies in your direction when you choose a bride. Until then, I will perform my motherly duties." She fluttered her lashes at him again.

He glanced in Miss Mary's direction. She was pressing her lips together as if she was either attempting not to laugh or trying to keep from speaking. Again, he wished that he could know what she was thinking. It was some time and several topics of discussion later before he was given an opportunity to speak to Mary without his mother keeping watch as she had gone to retrieve her list of soirees.

"You looked amused at my mother's desire to see me married," he commented.

She looked up at him from the book she seemed to be using as a shield against having to speak or even look at him.

"I am not unfamiliar with such a mother, though I admit I did not realize mothers of gentlemen put their sons forward in the same way mothers of young ladies do. You have seen and heard my mother."

He had. Mrs. Bennet was not shy about letting one and all know that she was looking for husbands for her daughters.

"And has your mother pushed you at anyone?" he asked.

Mary shook her head. "No, I have found that if I read sermons and refuse to admire lace, it confuses Mama. She has no clue what sort of gentleman would want such a strange girl." Her lips smiled but there was a touch of bitterness in her tone.

"Do you wish for her to be confused? Is that why you read sermons?"

"I find I like pondering the things found in sermons, but I also enjoy a novel or a book of poetry. However, I keep those for when I am alone in my room."

"Then, you do wish to confuse your mother." He leaned closer to her. This was the first conversation between them which did not include arguing and provoking. Even so, she was fascinating. He had never met a young lady who did not seem eager to have her mother promote her.

"Much like you, I do not wish to be pushed forward."

He chuckled. "Perhaps I should begin reading sermons," he teased.

And then, the most unexpected and enchanting thing happened. Miss Mary Bennet giggled. It was a sweet little chuckling sound that fit her. It was not high pitched and tittering as some young ladies giggled. There was no exaggerated covering of her lips with her hand. It was just a giggle which spilled out of her as easily as a gentle stream cascades over rocks.

"Your mother would send for the apothecary if you did," she teased in return.

He tipped his head and studied her. He had not entirely considered the fact that she might know how to tease. It was a lovely revelation, for if one could tease, then surely one could also flirt. The thought of flirting with Miss Mary was a tantalizing one.

"It would not fit who you are," she said uneasily. Her eyes watched his warily. "You are the antithesis to a sermon, my lord."

Her cheeks grew rosy. It was a lovely shade of pink, but it put a point on her words that pricked him.

"Do you really think of me so meanly?" he asked. She would likely never flirt with him if she considered him an utter reprobate.

She lowered her gaze. "I have seen little evidence to prove otherwise."

"Then, I challenge you."

Eyes filled with question met his.

"Find me a book of sermons to read, and I will read it so long as you refrain from reading anything but poetry or a novel for a week." He motioned toward the bookshelf. "Go on. Pick a book for me."

She glanced down at the book in her hand. "I surely would not even know if there is a book of sermons in this library. You may read this one. It is not a book of sermons, but it is also not a novel or poetry."

"But you are reading it," he protested.

She smiled, shook her head, and held the book out to him. "Not for a week, my lord."

Chapter 3

Wes flopped into a chair at his club and opened the curious book Miss Mary had given him. He could have gone home to read in peace, but he had not wished to be where nothing of interest might distract him from the task of reading this book.

A book on manners and rules of propriety for young ladies was not high on his list of texts to be read without interruption. In fact, he expected this to be a very dull sort of book to read, even if it might give a bit of insight into the female way of seeing things.

He flipped open the book.

A preface? No, he did not particularly care to know why the book was written.

He paged forward until he reached chapter one. Settling further into his chair, he stretched out his legs and tossed one ankle over the other as he began his arduous task of reading the book which had been assigned to him.

Mirror of The Graces

Preliminary Observations on the Subject.

In discoursing on the degree of consequence, in the scale of creation, that may be allowed to the human body, two extremes are generally adopted. – Epicureans, for obvious reasons, exalt our corporeal part to the first rank; and Stoics, by opposite deductions, degrade it to the last. But to neither of these opinions can the writer of these pages concede.

The body is as much a part of the human creature as the mind. It is the medium through which our souls see, feel, and act. By its outward expression of our internal thoughts, we convey to others a sense of our opinions, hopes, fears, and affections: we communicate love, we excite it.

Hmm. This book might not be so tiresome after all if it was to delve into the topic of exciting love.

We enjoy, not only the pleasure of the senses,

He smiled. Yes, yes, he did enjoy the pleasure of the senses.

But the delights that shoot from mind to mind, in the pressure of a hand, the glance of an eye, the whisper of the heart.

He looked up from the page he was reading, not to look at anything in particular, but to stare into the room as he considered that last phrase, *the whisper of the heart*. It was rather poetic and fanciful, but it was also something which had never seemed within his grasp. He had conducted more than one agreeable conversation with his eyes, and he would not wish to relinquish the pleasures that even the lightest touch of a hand might ignite. However, to hear one's heart call to another and then to have that call returned? Ah! That. That would be something worthy of the deprivation of the other two.

His mouth tipped into a crooked grin. He had felt it was so for some months now. Pleasure for pleasure's sake had become dull and familiar in a monotonous fashion. What was lacking, he had come to realize, while watching his brother and cousin when in Hertfordshire, was what this book so eloquently labelled *the whisper of the heart*.

What he desired, though he was not certain he was prepared to share it beyond the confines of his mind, was not some woman to warm his bed, but rather a woman – one woman, the same one, always – who would warm his bed, provide him with children, and sit beside him in the drawing room in the evening as they shared about their days or simply were in each other's presence.

He had been surprised when staying in Hertfordshire, without Clarice to visit when he wished for a tumble, that he had not missed such activities too overly much. The reason had been and, even now was, that he wanted what Darcy and Richard had found.

"Do not tell me you are reading on a fine day instead of riding in the park, taking in the view."

Lorcan Langley took the seat across from Wes.

"What book is it?" Wes's long-time friend asked.

Wes chuckled. "You'll think me daft."

"Too late, my friend. Most of us already think you to be so." Langley laughed and Wes joined him.

There was a certain delightful something which could be found in being unpredictable on occasions. It kept one's friends, as well as one's mother, on their toes.

"Be careful with that!" Wes cried when Langley snatched the book out of his hands. "It does not belong to me."

"I should hope not! *The Mirror of Graces*? A propriety guide? What are you about?" Langley turned the book over in his hands before opening it.

"I challenged a lady to read only novels or poetry for a week, and, in turn, she selected this book for me to read."

Langley's hands stilled with a page half-turned and half not as he looked up at Wes. "Are you attempting to seduce a bluestocking?"

"And if I am?" Wes countered.

Langley shook his head. "I would not have thought you would. Bluestockings are... well... intelligent." He smirked.

"And I am not?"

The question was met with a chuckle. "You are no idiot. You've bested me many times in school. It just seems a rather difficult task to convince an intelligent lady to..." He looked to his left and then his right and lowered his voice. "...to allow liberties without the prerequisite license."

"Difficult but not impossible."

Again, Langley chuckled. "Not for you, I suppose. If anyone can charm a lady out of her bluestockings, it is the Viscount Westonbury."

Wes nodded his head in acceptance of the compliment.

"Who is this fortunate young lady?"

"Someone I will not be charming out of her stocking or any other article of clothing." Unfortunately. For he would very much like to loosen the knot of hair on Miss Mary's head and watch those locks fall down around her shoulders as her dress slid to the floor.

"Then why are you reading her book?" Langley asked.

"Two reasons: she dislikes me, and she is a guest of my mother."

Langley's brow furrowed as he shook his head. "This is why we tend to think you daft. Why in the name of all that is green in a grassy garden are you even considering toying with a lady who dislikes you and is, I assume, liked by your mother. If you succeed in making the chit favor you, your mother will expect a marriage proposal for her guest and if you do not meet her expectations..." He shuddered.

Langley was not unfamiliar with the demanding and retribution-seeking nature of the Countess of Matlock. Upon the incident of Wes being locked out of his home and having his allowance removed for failure to pay a gambling debt, Langley's father had been sent a very direct letter about the dangers of gambling and the possible dissolution of the friendship between Wes and Langley if such a horrific lack of character were to persist in Mr. Langley's son.

"She locked me out of the house again — just today."

"Your mother did?"

Wes nodded. "She wanted to make a point about something having to do with her guests. I shall not be toying with either of them."

"There are two young ladies staying with your mother?" Langley's brows rose high.

"One of them shows promise of being her daughter and the other, the owner of this book, is that young lady's sister."

"Wait. You are not marrying, are you?"

Wes shook his head. "My brother is – or rather will be once he has healed."

"Do tell," Langley leaned forward, placed Miss Mary's book on his lap, and, resting his elbows on it, propped up his chin with his hands.

"You know Darcy is married, do you not?"

"Yes, yes, some lady from Hertfordshire whose sister married Charles Bingley after a spectacular compromise of Bingley's sister at the Johnson's ball. I say, I have never seen the likes of it. It was very well done. If I had not heard Mr. Johnson whispering about how it had all been arranged, I would have thought it a fabulous accident. I cannot say I ever suspected Darcy would go to such lengths to help his friend."

Of course, Langley knew more details about the event than most would. The man was positively brilliant at being in the right place at the right time. And he was not wrong that the compromise had been, and still was, shocking. The change which had come over Darcy in the past few months was remarkable.

"He was not only helping his friend," Wes said. "He was hoping to gain the favour of the lady who is now his wife."

"Then, it appears it was a beautifully executed plan."

"Indeed. Who knew Darcy was capable of such?"

"It seems you are not the only member of your family capable of charming a difficult to charm lady."

Wes chuckled. "So it seems."

"Now about how this all relates to your brother," Langley prompted.

"Darcy's wife has four sisters."

"And..." Langley's look was expectant.

This was why Wes had been able to best the man on several occasions. Langley did not lack for intelligence, but his intelligence was not of the rapid variety.

"My mother's houseguests are two of Mrs. Darcy's sisters."

Langley's eyes grew wide. "Your brother is not marrying an heiress?"

Wes shook his head. "She might not have bags of money, but Lori, I have not seen the likes of it. The way she cares for him and can suggest something, and he hurries to do it."

"Your brother?"

Wes nodded.

"But he never does anything unless he wants to."

"Until now. Mother is, of course, in her glory since Miss Lydia's ideas seem to blend effortlessly with those of my mother, and that is why Miss Lydia and her sister Miss Mary are currently ensconced at Matlock House. Mother wished for an ally in seeing that my brother recovers properly." He leaned forward and whispered. "She has him taking a nap every day."

"Your mother?"

Wes sighed. "Do try to keep up, Lori. Not my mother, Miss Lydia. I told you, she speaks, and Richard does. Then again, if we had ladies such as her batting their lashes at us, we would likely be just as compliant."

"She is pretty then?"

"Very."

"And her sister who is with her?"

"In a spinsterly sort of fashion, yes." He gave his friend a pointed look. "That book has found its perfect audience in her hands. Buttons to her throat. Not a wayward tress. And very little lace. It all creates a very plain sort of appearance."

Langley smiled. "But if it was all undone?"

Wes blew out a breath. "She'd have to employ footmen to keep the swains away."

"And you are *not* attempting to seduce her?" Langley asked with a laugh.

"No." Wes was not even sure he was capable of doing so if he were to attempt it.

"Because of your mother?"

Wes nodded. "And the fact that Miss Mary does

not like me." He chuckled. "Do you know that on our first meeting, she scolded me most severely for my behaviour." He shrugged. "She had heard tales about me and does not approve of places like Sally's."

"She knows about Sally's?"

Wes rose. "Come. This is not the place for such conversations, and I must inform you that if any of what I tell you is ever shared elsewhere, I shall not call you out but will simply leave you to my mother to do with as she sees fit."

Langley laughed. "You know I never tell your tales, but I hear the weight of your word. I would not for a moment wish to have my fate placed in the hands of Lady Matlock. I'd rather you shoot me."

Chapter 4

Two days later, Wes's prediction that Miss Mary would look far from plain if she were to loosen her hair and wear a different style of dress became fact. Beautiful, enticing, alluring fact which caused him to find his jaw in need of snapping closed when Miss Mary and Miss Lydia descended the stairs at Matlock House to join him, his mother, and his father so that they might all depart for the musicale he was not looking forward to attending.

"Rich—" Wes's voice cracked, and he cleared his throat. "Richard is not joining us?" he managed to ask in a rather normal sounding tone. He wished to look toward his father, but his eyes would not leave Mary.

"Not tonight," his father replied. "His scar holds him back as much as his head."

Wes nodded as if he was actually interested in the answer to his question.

What had his mother done to Miss Mary? Her hair was piled loosely on her head with a few curls arranged in a becoming fashion to frame her face, and her dress was neither somber in color nor fit. Had he ever seen a lady with a complexion so well-suited to that shade of pink?

Lady Matlock coughed softly, and Wes darted a guilty look at her. However, it was not he who was the subject of his mother's displeasure.

"The lace." Lady Matlock extended her hand in Mary's direction.

Surely, she was not seriously going to make Mary discard that lace, was she? The neckline of Miss Mary's dress was tantalizing enough with the lace where it was.

Mary drew and released a breath in a heavy sigh as she did what Wes feared she would and removed the lace she had tucked into her dress to cover herself.

The effect was pleasing, but...

"One must display herself to best advantage," Lady Matlock instructed. "We must not leave the gentleman wondering about your womanly qualities."

Good heavens! Was he truly supposed to stand here and listen to his mother lecture the beguiling Miss Mary about displaying her delectably creamy and not insignificant assets?

"Do you really think that is necessary?" Wes asked. "The night is cool. We would not wish for Miss Mary to catch a chill."

His mother chuckled. "No, we would not wish for that, so she will wear a wrap while outside. However, you know how warm these events can become. There is no danger of Miss Bennet catching a chill without this bit of lace." She handed the lace she held to her maid who stood ready with wraps for the ladies. "There is, however, the danger of her not catching a husband if she wears the lace."

"Are you telling me that you wish for your charge to be snapped up by some gentleman who only wishes to get a better look at her breasts?" He grimaced as Miss Mary and Miss Lydia gasped in unison.

"Reginald," his father scolded.

"Forgive me. I forgot I was not speaking privately to my mother."

"Really, Reginald, I would not have taken you for a prude," his mother replied as she accepted help with her outerwear. "This is how things are, you know. A lady must entice the gentleman to spend time with her. If she does it by arousing his desires, she does it by arousing his desires. Surely you are not unaware of these things — this game we must play."

"But Miss Mary is not accustomed to the ways of the ton," Wes protested.

"But she will be. Your mother is a fine teacher," Lord Matlock said. "And I do not see anything indecent with how Miss Bennet is dressed. She looks exceptionally pretty."

Downright enticingly beautiful would be a better way to say it.

"Do you not agree?" Lady Matlock asked him. "You have yet to compliment either Miss Bennet or Miss Lydia on how they look." She tipped her head and gave him a stern look. "I expected better from you."

He sighed and took a moment to look at Miss Lydia who was wearing a blue creation that was equally as lovely though not as eye-catching as the pink frock with burgundy trim on her sister. "You both look beautiful. I apologize for my oversight."

Mary pursed her lips. "Is that so? Do we actually look beautiful, or are you simply saying what you must? Is this part of the game?"

"You look da—" He cut off his curse with a smile when his mother cleared her throat. "You look beautiful."

He extended his arm to Miss Mary who was now safely ensconced in her wrap with only a bit of creamy white flesh peeking out at her collarbone.

"I find myself surprised by your objection to my dress," she said to him as they followed Lord and Lady Matlock to the carriage.

"I am surprised you would wear such a dress," he returned. "Why are you?"

"Because one wears what one is told to wear when the guest of Lady Matlock."

He chuckled. "The same is true if one is a son of Lady Matlock. However, that is not what I meant. Why are you surprised by my objection to your dress? I cannot imagine you are comfortable in such a garb. It is not like how I have seen you dress."

"Do you think me incapable of wearing such revealing garments?"

She was using that tone she used when she was about to launch into some argument with him, and rather than causing him to proceed with caution, it tempted him to provoke her further. "Yes."

"Well, I am not." She wiggled her shoulders and allowed her wrap to fall onto her upper arms.

Fabulous! As much as the action and resulting bare shoulders were delectable, he feared he had managed to provoke her into pretending to be comfortable with exposing her fair flesh to one and all. Oddly, that thought bothered him.

"As to my surprise at your objection," she continued in that same sharp, annoyed tone. "I would think that a gentleman of your ilk would prefer all ladies to have their wares on display so that it would be easier for him to pick which one he would use tonight."

"Mary!" Lydia scolded. "I will write to Papa."

Mary turned a cunning smile on her sister before it was time for Wes to hand her into the carriage. "If I go home, so do you."

Lydia's mouth dropped open.

"Is that what you want?" Mary asked with a flutter of lashes.

If he had not witnessed it, Wes would never have believed that Miss Mary was capable of being so devious. Perhaps she was not so prim and proper as she appeared.

"I do not use women," he whispered.

He could see the flare of anger in her eyes when she turned toward him.

"Then, you are married to whatever her name is at Sally's house? Do you see to her care? Will she be the mother of your children?"

"Of course, not."

"Precisely. You use her for your own gratification and care not what happens to her beyond that." She took the hand of the footman next to the carriage and climbed in, leaving Wes without the option of refuting her words or the privilege of seeing her into the vehicle.

Instead, he was left to glare after her. If his father was not in the carriage, he might have told her that he paid Clarice handsomely, and that he treated her well, and that he knew she lacked for nothing under Sally's care.

"She is dreadful at times," Miss Lydia apologized.

"I do not use women," he said once again to Lydia. Perhaps he could convince just one Miss Bennet. "It is a business arrangement." What was wrong with a business arrangement?

Lydia only shrugged and smiled at him sadly before she also entered the carriage.

Apparently, neither Miss Bennet was disposed to thinking well of him. Wes shook his head and looked skyward before taking a deep, somewhat calming, breath and taking his place next to his father on the carriage bench.

~*~*~

"Do you think you could attempt to look pleased to be here?" Lady Matlock asked behind her fan as they took their seats to wait for the night of music to begin.

"No," Wes grumbled, his scowl deepening. He still wished to argue his point with Miss Mary, and, though she was seated at his side, he knew better than to continue or start any argument while under the scrutiny of the ton.

"Everyone will think you disapprove of my guests," his mother added.

At present, he did. Well, not both of her guests. Just one. The fiery demon in the pink dress next to him.

"Westonbury," his father said in a soft rumble.

"I will attempt to look pleased," Wes assured his mother. It would not be an easy feat, but he was not completely unequal to the challenge.

And for the entire first half of the evening, he wore a smile and nodded and clapped just as would be expected, while all the while understanding more and more why his mother was so concerned about appearances tonight. There was not a person in the room who had not, at one point or another, peeked inquisitively at their party. Some had merely glanced in their direction with a raised brow, while other had added a whispered conversation after scrutinizing the Miss Bennets.

As the intermission began, he drew and released a breath quietly, summoning his reserve of patience and pleasantness. He would be more than equal to the challenge of looking as if he was enjoying himself. He would enjoy himself, and in so doing, he would prove Miss Mary wrong. He would demonstrate to her that he actually cared for the wellbeing of every lady he met, beginning with her and her sister.

The ton would not see Miss Mary or Miss Lydia as less than acceptable if he could help it. They would see that not only his parents but also he both accepted and approved of the Miss Bennets. After all, Miss Mary's and Miss Lydia's acceptance was important to his brother, and he would not harm Richard in any fashion. Not now. Not ever.

He smiled and, for the first time since arriving, relaxed into his chair, feeling quite delighted that aiding his brother would come with the added bonus of proving Miss Mary wrong.

Chapter 5

"How was the musicale?" Richard stood at the top of the staircase, leaning on the wall as if he had been waiting there for some time for his parents and the Miss Bennets to return home.

"Why are you still awake?" Lydia countered.

"I could not sleep without knowing how your first foray into society went," he replied.

"It was an excellent introduction," Lady Matlock called up to him. "I am certain our Miss Lydia will be the talk of the town by tomorrow." She held up a hand and turned from looking up the stairs to where her butler stood near the door. "Some wine and cheese in the library, if you will, Nibley." She looked at Wes and sighed. "I suppose you can join us if you behave."

To Mary's surprise, Wes shook his head.

"I should go home."

His tone was almost despondent. Mary's eyebrow cocked in interest.

"That is what you told Langley you were going to do," Lord Matlock commented.

"Langley was there?" Richard asked. "I have not seen him in an age."

"He is very handsome," Lydia said. "Is he not, Mary?"

Mary felt her face flush. "He is." Very handsome. "And amiable."

"Yes, amiable," Wes muttered, his lips curling in disgust.

Was not Mr. Langley a good friend of Lord Westonbury? Why would he sneer at a friend? Mary rolled her eyes. Why was she even wondering such a thing? Of course, Lord Westonbury would sneer at a friend. He had very little sense of how to behave appropriately. She should not be surprised by his words and expression. It was how he was. He played at being proper when he must, but when he was at leisure, he was... well... quite the opposite.

"Are you sure you cannot have just one glass of wine with us?" his mother asked.

Again, Wes shook his head and refused. However, this time, his eyes lingered on Mary before he turned away toward the door.

"He seems out of sorts," Lord Matlock muttered.

"I must say it is unlike him to refuse a glass of wine," Lady Matlock agreed.

"He has not been right all evening," Lord Matlock continued as they ascended the stairs behind Lydia and Mary. "He does not usually require scolding into being personable."

Lady Matlock sighed. "As much as I tease him about misbehaving, he is, for the most part, good, even if he is a bit of a rapscallion at times."

Lord Matlock chuckled. "At times? That boy has always had a penchant for finding trouble or as he called it a bit of fun."

"Maybe he will outgrow it someday."

Lady Matlock's tone sounded light and teasing to Mary.

"I doubt it," Lord Matlock replied. "You have not, and he is a good deal like his mother."

Out of the corner of her eye, as she turned to go to the library, she saw Lord Matlock lift his wife's hand to his lips. The gesture caused her cheeks to warm and her heart to sigh for it was so intimate and lovely.

She had come to know a little about her hosts in the few days she had been at Matlock House. Lady Matlock was always busy doing something. She was rarely still. There were menus to approve, a room that was in want of some new furnishings, two guests who must – simply must – have new gowns, and then, there were her sons who seemed to be her favorite topic of conversation. Lord Matlock, on the other hand, despite being somewhat of a tease, was quieter in nature, willing to watch and listen before inserting his opinion on anything. He also had a tendency to look austere and foreboding when contemplating things. His brow would furrow, and his lips would purse in a small scowl. They were different in many ways, but those differences seemed to complement the other perfectly.

"Mary was rude."

Mary's head snapped toward her sister. "Lydia," she hissed. She did not care if Lydia was just whispering to Colonel Fitzwilliam. What if Lord and Lady Matlock heard her?

"You were," Lydia replied. "She accused your brother of using women."

"Lydia," Mary hissed again with a tip of her head toward Lord and Lady Matlock.

"You will not let me write to Papa," Lydia continued, her eyes narrowing.

"Very well, I was rude. Now, please do not speak of it anymore."

"But I should like to," Richard said.

Mary shook her head.

"Not now, I understand, but maybe at another time? I would just like to know your reasoning is all, nothing more."

Mary sighed and took a seat near Lydia. "It would be most improper, just as it was for me to have mentioned it at all, to begin with. I should moderate my displeasure and keep my thoughts to myself." She glanced furtively toward the door through which Lord and Lady Matlock were just entering.

"Do you know," Lady Matlock said to the room as she took a seat, "Mrs. Salter was not even present." She shook her head. "I was hoping she would be."

Marys' brow furrowed. Why would Lady Matlock wish to see Mrs. Salter? As far as Mary was concerned, the woman was dreadful and the less which was seen of her, the better.

"I have heard a thing or two about the lady,"

Lady Matlock said, reading the question in Mary's expression. "She seems to think very highly of herself."

"Indeed, she does," Mary agreed.

"I thought," Lady Matlock continued, "it would be delightful for her to see two of her rival's daughters in my company." Her eyebrows flicked upward quickly. "I have heard she disparaged your mother, though I do not know the full tale."

Lord Matlock put a hand on his wife's arm. She smiled at him and turned the subject.

"The music was, for the most part, wonderful. Miss Johnson played the harp, but your brother refused to congratulate her on a job well done."

"Only because you suggested it," Lord Matlock inserted.

"Oh, but he did tell her she had played well," Lydia cried. "I heard him. It was just before introducing Mary and me to her."

"Indeed?" An excessively surprised Lord Matlock looked to Mary for confirmation.

Mary nodded. Lord Westonbury had made a point of introducing them to several young ladies he deemed worthy of the introduction, and he had spoken kindly to each person as he did so.

"She is a dear girl," Lady Matlock said. "If only she had a bit more spine, I might truly push Reginald in her direction, but sadly, she is too sweet for him."

Mary closed her mouth and pressed her lips together to keep her thoughts contained where they should be. Had not Lady Matlock suggested her son pursue Miss Johnson? Why would a mother suggest a particular lady as a possible bride when she did not think that the lady and her son would suit? Either Lady Matlock was more like her mother than Mary wished to admit, for until this moment, she had considered Lady Matlock to be rather sensible, or it must be part of the game Lady Matlock had referred to earlier tonight before they had left the house.

"I truly have not found a lady in town who is worthy of him," Lady Matlock continued.

Lord Matlock chuckled. "You mean a lady who could handle him."

Lady Matlock shrugged and smiled. "I suppose one could say it that way. He was never an easy child, and he has not lost his ambition. However, it does want some guidance, but we are not here to discuss such things." She smiled at Mary. "I am

sure that someday Reginald will find a lady to challenge him appropriately."

"As you do, my love?" Lord Matlock's lips were
curled into a smile that said he already knew the
answer to the question.

Mary could not help but smile at the exchange.
She had not thought that people of rank could be
so regular. They wore fine clothes, commanded an
army of servants, and lived sumptuously, but for
all the accouterments their station afforded them,
when in private, Lord and Lady Matlock were not
so very different from her own parents – teasing
and speaking of seeing their children well-settled.

Lady Matlock winked at her husband and then
turned back to Mary. "I think Mr. Langley holds
some promise. I almost completely approve of
him."

Mary's eyes grew wide. "You mean for me?"

"Yes, dear, for you. Miss Lydia is already
attached."

"Mr. Langley?' Mary questioned. "As in Lord
Westonbury's friend?"

"Yes, dear, that Mr. Langley. I know of no other.
Do you have an objection to him?"

Mary pressed her lips together. How was she to state her objection without offending?

"He is handsome," Mary finally said after a moment of contemplation while the room sat uncomfortably silent, "but I know little of his character."

Lady Matlock sighed. "That is always the issue, is it not? But it is not without a solution. You will just have to discover what you can of his character when he comes to call on you tomorrow."

Had she heard that correctly? "He is coming to call on me tomorrow? Me?"

"Yes, dear."

Well, that was a new thing! Gentlemen did not call at Longbourn to see her. They had always come to see Lydia and Kitty or Jane. She and Lizzy had only ever been ornaments in the sitting room or chaperones on walks. She was not entirely certain she knew how to be called on.

"How does one do that?" She blushed as her thoughts slipped out of her mouth.

"How does one do what?" Lady Matlock asked.

Wonderful. Mary clasped her hands together firmly. Now she was going to have to admit her forlorn status to a countess. Was it not bad enough that everyone in Meryton expected her to be a spinster? Did she really need to confess such a thing to Lady Matlock?

"Mary has never had a suitor," Lydia supplied.

Mary scowled at her sister.

"Oh, is that all?" Lady Matlock waved the concern away. "Every lady starts somewhere. You are not so very old. Nineteen is a fine age to begin. Why I was not married until I was twenty, and my husband was my only suitor."

"But you are beautiful." The words were out of Mary's mouth before she could think better of it.

Lady Matlock laughed. "And so are you when you allow yourself to be."

"Had my wife made her debut in town, I am certain she would have had a battalion of suitors," Lord Matlock said. "However, she did not make her debut in town, and she is not a standard order ton approved lady, which speaks in part to her wish to see the likes of Mrs. Salter put in her place." He took his wife's hand again. "I actually had to travel all the way to Scotland just to find her."

"Scotland?" Lydia cried. "But you do not sound Scottish."

Lady Matlock laughed. "I am not. My father had

died, you see. His estate passed to my uncle, and my uncle thought that it was far better that I take a position as a companion than attend school. As he saw it, I could learn all I needed to about how to behave as a proper lady while earning my keep and costing him not a cent."

"Fortunately, years earlier, my great aunt had married a Scottish landowner," Lord Matlock added. "And when he died, she had the great good sense to employ the prettiest companion I have ever seen."

"You were a companion?" Lydia was all astonishment and Mary could not blame her. "Yet, you married an earl?"

Lady Matlock shrugged. "He was merely a viscount at the time. The Viscount Westonbury."

Lydia's mouth opened and then closed.

"What is it?" Lady Matlock asked.

Lydia shook her head. "It is silly."

"Nothing that makes a lady's brow furrow as yours is now is too silly to ask," Lady Matlock assured her.

Mary hoped that was true, and from the way Lydia bit her lip and laced her fingers together in her lap, she was mostly confident that Lydia's question would not be entirely improper for there seemed to be a great deal of thought going into it.

"It is just something Lady Catherine said," Lydia said softly.

"Ah, I see," Lord Matlock said with a knowing smile. "My sister was not fond of my choice of bride, and I suspect she voiced her displeasure about your status. Is that it?"

Lydia nodded.

"As long as the lady, whom my son loves, loves him in return and will do him good and not ill, status is of little importance to me," Lord Matlock explained with a kind smile for Lydia. "Within reason, of course. I would discourage either of my sons from marrying too far beneath them. There is much to know in order to circulate in the sphere in which they live. However, the daughter of a gentleman, even if she is a companion to a surly old woman, is not beneath either their notice or mine. We are pleased to gain you as a daughter." He winked at Mary. "You are welcome to my other son if you wish."

Horror washed over Mary and must have been etched in her features for Lord Matlock laughed and added, "He is truly not so bad as he seems, however, I can understand he is perhaps not the sort of gentleman for whom you would wish."

"It is not that I do not like him," Mary hastened to cover her uncensored reaction. "It is just that we would not suit, my lord."

"Oh, not at all," Lady Matlock agreed with a smile. "You and he are very like night and day."

She rose as a tray of meat, cheese, and rolls was placed on a table with a bottle of wine. "Finally," she said, and the current conversation was forgotten in favour of wine and food.

Chapter 6

The clouds were hanging rather low the morning after the musicale as Wes rode toward the park. It would likely rain, which would make for less of a crowd on Rotten Row, and fewer people to whom he had to appear to be friendly suited Wes quite well. His sleep last night had been fitful at best, and today, he had not been able to focus on his work, nor had he been able to comprehend a word he read from that blasted book without reading it three times over. His mind was not what it should be, and he knew precisely what — or rather who — was the cause of his unsettled state.

He pulled out his watch. Calling hours would begin soon. He would ride until they were over, and then, he would make an appearance at Matlock House to glean what he could about Langley's call.

Langley. His lips curled in displeasure as he

shook his head. Of all the gentlemen who were in London and to whom Miss Mary had been introduced, it had to be Langley who was to be favoured with Miss Mary's approval.

If it were any other gentleman, there would be a hope of not having to bear with some sort of manufactured indifference the tales of a lover's hopeful pursuit. It would be dreadful enough to have to hear his mother exclaim over Miss Mary's good fortune. But as it was, he would also have to endure Langley's raptures.

He should turn around and ride to Matlock House instead of the park. He had a few tales he could tell Miss Mary about Lorcan Langley. The man might seem all that was charming and noble, but he was no angel. Clarice knew Langley. True, she did not know him as well as she knew Wes, but the fact remained that she did know him, and if Miss Mary did not approve of him for having visited Sally's, then she would most certainly not approve of Langley either if she knew.

The only thing which was keeping him at this very moment from sharing all he knew about his friend was a desire to not be seen as a jealous and desperate schoolboy. And that thought was even more disturbing than the idea of Langley succeeding with Miss Mary. When was the last time he had been jealous? There was very little over which Wes ever felt envious.

He nodded to a gentleman and his lady who were riding in a carriage with the top up to fend off the coming rain.

The last time Wes remembered feeling jealous was when Richard got a new horse that proved to be of far better stock than any Wes had ever owned to that point. He had quelled that bout of envy by eventually finding and purchasing a stallion that was equal to Richard's. While such a thing had worked well then, he could not just go out and purchase a lady equal to Miss Mary — firstly, because she was a lady and not a horse, and secondly, though likely most importantly, because he was certain there was no lady equal to Miss Mary. She was a one-of-a-kind treasure. There was not a single female of his acquaintance whom he could think of who wore buttons to her throat and scowled at any hint of impropriety. In fact, every lady he knew would happily overlook any perceived bad behaviour on his part simply because of his title and wealth. Mary, however, cared not one whit about his rank. She valued what, in her opinion, he did not possess – an honourable character.

He shook his head. He had performed his role of proper gentleman quite well last night at the musicale. He had been polite. He had introduced Mary and Lydia to several people. He had crowed about his delight in having secured such lovely young ladies as relations thanks to his cousin's marriage. And what did such commendable behaviour get him? Nothing. Not one single thing. However, it did earn Langley a seat in the green drawing room.

He nudged his horse to go faster. He wanted to gallop. He wanted to feel the beast beneath him pounding the earth in a punishing flurry of hooves. But he would not satisfy his desire for the same reason he had not made his way to Sally's since returning to town. Mary would not approve.

"Westonbury!"

Wes turned to see that it was Darcy's carriage which had approached. He sighed and nodded his greeting to each of the occupants once both his horse and Darcy's carriage had come to a stop.

"I had not thought to see you out driving," Wes said to Darcy.

"Ah, but I have sisters and a wife who must see and be seen."

"It is not a very good day for it," Wes commented, looking at the darkening clouds.

"But the canopy can be put into place quickly," Darcy assured him. "You, on the other hand, will be fortunate to arrive home without being thoroughly soaked."

"I think I can manage a bit of a drenching."

"How is Richard?" Georgiana asked. "And Mary and Lydia?"

"Richard is doing well. He can read a bit now and is considering making his way into society for an event or two. Miss Mary and Miss Lydia have already ventured into society. They attended a musicale with my mother and father last night."

"Did they?" Kitty asked eagerly. "I should love to attend a musicale."

"Was it a successful venture?" There was a note of concern in Elizabeth's tone.

Wes nodded. "I believe it was. Mr. Langley is expected to call on Miss Mary today." He was likely at Matlock House as they spoke. The thought caused him to clench his jaw shut tightly.

"You do not seem very pleased about that," Darcy said.

Wes smiled a forced and false smile. "Why would I not be anything less than pleased?" His eyes held Darcy's for a long silent minute before Darcy replied.

"That is the question, is it not?"

"It appears to be," Wes answered.

"Why are you displeased?" Darcy asked.

Why? Because Miss Mary approved of anyone and everyone save him, because he was supposed to be the one sitting in the green drawing room talking to Miss Mary, and because he did not wish to share her with the likes of Langley. Of course, he was barely able to admit such things to himself, so there was no way on God's green earth that he was going to admit it to Darcy.

Was shook his head. "I am not displeased. I am delighted. Langley is a good friend." For now. "However, it is a bit of a dreary day, and I think the clouds have not remained in the sky as they should but have settled on my mood."

"It is excessively easy to be out of sorts on a cloudy day," Kitty agreed.

Fantastic. Now he was not a just jealous school-boy, but also a temperamental fool.

"A ride is often just the thing to lift my spirits," he assured Kitty. "So, I best get back to it."

"Do try to avoid the rain," Mrs. Darcy cautioned. "Getting caught out in it can lead to a miserable few days in bed."

"I will do my best to stay well. I thank you for your concern." At the moment, he did not care if he was laid up with sniffles and chills. He already felt rather miserable. At least, if he were ill, then, he would have a good reason for it.

~*~*~

"Reginald!" his mother cried upon seeing his drenched state a bit less than two hours later.

"I am seeing that a dry set of clothes are made ready for him, my lady," Nibley assured Lady Matlock before Wes could say a word.

"While you are waiting, do not drip on the rug or the furniture," his mother scolded.

"I have no intention of dripping on anything other than this portion of the floor." He smiled as she shook her head. "It was a refreshing ride. I saw Darcy and Mrs. Darcy as well as Miss Kitty and Georgiana."

"Did you invite them to call on me?" his mother asked.

"You forget, madame, that I do not live here, and it would be rather rude of me to invite them to a home that is not mine."

Lady Matlock huffed.

"Did I miss Langley?" he asked while watching Miss Mary, who other than a faint blush seemed very good at concealing her feelings about the gentleman.

"Yes," his mother replied.

"And was he as handsome and amiable as he was last night?"

Mary rolled her eyes. That seemed to be an affirmative response.

"He usually –" Wes paused to sneeze, "is. Or so I have heard from more than one lady." He pushed his mother's hand away from his forehead. "I am well. It was merely a sneeze."

Her answering look said she was not convinced of the fact. "How long were you in the rain?"

Wes shook his head. "How long has it been raining?"

His mother clucked her tongue. "Go find Nibley and some dry clothing." She shook her head. "This is why you need a wife. Someone must see to your care." Her hand was once again on his forehead. "You will stay for dinner."

There was no refusing the tone she used, though Wes did consider doing so just because he was still feeling ornery. However, he knew better than to push too far when it came to his mother and her need to see her children were well. Therefore, he stayed for dinner as instructed, and all through their meal, Wes valiantly attempted to refrain from sneezing, but as is sometimes the case, his valiant effort was not successful.

"I can convalesce in my room in Brook Street," Wes protested as his mother gave instructions for a few things to be brought to Matlock House for Wes, who she had decided was not leaving until she knew he was well. "Do you forget you have guests? You would not wish for one of them to become ill."

His mother raised an eyebrow at him and left the drawing room, most likely to see that his room was made ready for him. Hopefully, she was not also sending for the apothecary. It was only a sniffle... and a mild aching in his shoulders.

"Why would you ride in the rain?" Lord Matlock asked as he settled into a chair with a book.

Wes shrugged. "It seemed a good idea at the time. I thought it would clear away some of my foul mood."

"And did it work?" Richard asked from his place at the card table.

Wes shook his head. How could it have? Langley had still called on Mary and from what he had heard during dinner, it had been a successful call. They were to go driving tomorrow if it was a fine day. Worst of all, Mary seemed to be happy about the arrangement. He rose and crossed to stand in front of the fire and next to where Mary sat, hiding behind a book.

"Did you ask him about brothels?" Wes whispered to Mary.

"I beg your pardon?"

"Langley. Did you ask him about brothels?"

Mary's brow furrowed. "Why should I?"

"It was part of our first conversation, so I assumed..." he let the thought trail off. Oh, his head was beginning to throb. It seemed as if his wish to have a reason to be miserable was to come true. "You should ask him."

"Why would I do that?" Mary hissed.

Wes shrugged. "He knows Sally, but perhaps it is only I who is to be condemned for such things."

"Lydia is my sister."

It was Wes's turn to be confused. "Yes, I know."

"You treated her like... well... like she was one of Sally's girls."

Wes cast a glance toward his father who seemed not to have heard Mary's whisper, which was not as soft as it had been a moment ago. "I did not know who she was." Had he not said as much in their first conversation about this subject?

"So you have said, and yet you do not or will not see your error. Do you know who any of them are? Who are their sisters? Who are their brothers, their fathers, their mothers?"

"I know some," he answered, causing her eyebrows to lift. Somehow, it appeared that such a reply had made her despise him more and not less.

She closed her book and rose. "I think I will find something different to read," she said to the room. "I will return." However, before she left, it seemed she had one more thing to say to him because she stepped closer to him and lowered her voice. "You know, Wickham knew who my sisters were and still used them ill."

"Wickham is a cad." He rubbed the spot between his eyes that was pounding.

"And how are you any better, my lord?" she whispered before taking her leave.

Chapter 7

"What did you say to Lord Westonbury?" Lydia asked later that night as she and Mary were preparing for bed. "He looked worse than miserable when you left the drawing room."

"I cannot tell you." Mary glanced over her shoulder toward Lydia from where she sat brushing her hair.

"I promise not to tell Papa," Lydia begged, climbing closer to the end of the bed and to where Mary was sitting.

"You will scold me." And she knew she would deserve it, for she had let her displeasure overpower her resolve to hold her tongue once again. She was a guest at Matlock House, and Papa had cautioned her that not holding her tongue, even when presented with things she found reprehensible, posed a danger to both of her sisters being well-accepted in the ton. Thankfully, her lack of restraint had once again occurred at Matlock House when there were no visitors present. However, according to how she had been thinking since that small outburst, it mattered very little where it occurred. Giving in to one's emotions and allow them to have control of one's manners was forming a bad habit. Habits which were born at home might eventually spill over into every area of a young lady's life, and that would be most disastrous.

"Were you talking about brothels again?" Lydia whispered.

Mary pressed her lips together.

"I will not scold. I promise."

"I do not think that is a promise you will be able to keep."

"Then you were speaking of brothels!"

Mary pulled in a deep breath and expelled it as she began to braid her hair. "He asked me if I had asked Mr. Langley about brothels."

"He did not!" Lydia's chin was propped up on her hands as she lay on her stomach watching Mary.

"He did. He is most improper."

"He has never been improper to me," Lydia argued. "Just you." Her face scrunched. "And his mother and Mr. Darcy and the colonel." She paused. Her face was still scrunched up in thought. "I believe that is it. You and a few of his family members. He was all that was proper at the musicale."

Mary turned to look at Lydia. "Do you not see the trouble with that? He is one thing in one place and another thing altogether in another place."

"So is Jane," Lydia replied. "She is far more teasing at home than at an assembly."

"Teasing is not the same as being utterly improper." Mary's lips pursed and her brow furrowed with displeasure. "He visits brothels."

"Brothels? Are you sure it is more than one?" Lydia batted her lashes and smirked.

"Oh, do not be ridiculous, Lydia. You know what I meant. He has a mistress."

Lydia did not respond immediately. She merely looked at Mary for a long minute. "Is that why you dislike him? Because he has a mistress?"

Mary nodded. "In part." She tied the end of her braid with a ribbon. "Such relations between a man and a woman should only be enjoyed in marriage. That is what the parson would say, and you know it."

Lydia scooted over as Mary joined her on the bed.

"But it is more than that." She sighed. "I am not even certain I can explain it properly."

"I am not good at explaining many things. I will not make fun of you."

Mary smiled at Lydia. "You have changed and for the better."

"How do you mean?"

"You would not tease me for making a mess of an explanation, would you?"

Lydia shook her head.

"But," Mary continued, "just three months ago, you would have." She chuckled. "And three months ago, I would not have feared you scolding me for behaving less than properly." She shrugged. "I think I like this new Lydia – at least, when she is not scolding me, I do."

Lydia wore a pleased smile. "Then you will explain to me why you do not like Lord Weston-bury?"

Mary blew out a great breath. "I will try." She arranged herself more comfortably on the bed. "I do not like it when people do not see me for who I am. I have been belittled and ridiculed quite often over the years."

Lydia gasped. "Oh, I think I must apologize for that, for I am certain I was one of those people."

"You were," Mary admitted, "but you were not alone." She paused. The sting of being thought of as less than others or being spoken of as a future spinster, for who could love a girl like Mary, hung like a millstone on her heart. It always had, but she had managed to hide it away behind sardonic comments and a seemingly undaunted façade. She could bear it for herself to a point, but she feared she either had reached the end of her ability to forebear or could not bear to see others – especially her sisters – treated in such a fashion – and by a stranger no less!

"I cannot approve of someone who willingly, and for pleasure's sake, will not offer the respect due to another human being simply because they are a fellow human being."

Lydia's brow was furrowed. Why was it so hard to explain?

"I long for respect, to be loved for who I am, and to be treated as if I matter and am more than just someone to order about or use as a joke." Mary blinked against the tears which gathered in her eyes. "And I will not sit idly by and nod and smile when someone treats my sisters in such a fashion. I was delighted to see the bruises on Mr. Wickham's face when we met him in Meryton when shopping with Miss Darcy. I do not oppose the colonel or Mr. Darcy using force against a gentleman who has treated my sisters so ill – not to mention what he has done to Miss Darcy!" She could feel the anger she had suppressed for so long welling up inside of her and begging to be released. "And I would very much have liked to have slapped Lord West-onbury's face both at that brothel and at Nether-field when he offered you a coin for a kiss. I would still like to slap him, and I know that is not right. However, I would! There. I have said it. I have admitted the ugliness of my heart."

Lydia sat up and put an arm around Mary's shoulder.

"But I cannot slap him with anything more than my words," she added in a whisper.

"He did not offer me a coin at Sally's. I asked for one," Lydia said softly as she squeezed Mary close.

"But he asked you for a kiss because he thought

you were... one of them. He did not think for a moment that you might be a lady worthy of respect. I do not know if I can forgive that even though I know I likely should."

She blew out another great breath. "And now he has told me that Mr. Langley, who seems so very nice, is little better." She looked at Lydia. "He said Mr. Langley knows Sally." She shook her head at the hopelessness she felt. "Is it too much to ask that I be able to marry a gentleman who has loved me and no other in the way that a husband loves his wife?"

"I am not Jane," Lydia said softly. "I am sure I do not know the answer to that."

"But you have found such a gentleman, have you not?"

Lydia shrugged. "I have never asked."

"But do you not worry about such a thing?"

Lydia shook her head.

"How can you not?" Mary knew that some ladies seemed to care little about the faithfulness of their husbands. She had heard the tales of such women from Lady Lucas and Mrs. Long. However, she also knew that her father had never strayed from his vows to her mother. She supposed a wife had very little to do but accept a husband's wayward ways, but she did not wish to be such a wife. She longed for what her mother had with her father – a love that endured and was true, a love which never wavered – and in her mind, the surest way to guarantee such a happy future was to marry a gentleman who had never developed a taste for promiscuity.

"I have never thought to worry about such a thing. Do you think I should?" Lydia scooted so that she was facing Mary. "I know that the colonel seems very loyal to all those he loves, and since he loves me, I trust he will be loyal to me in all ways. Is that wrong?"

Mary lifted a shoulder and let it drop. It did not sound wrong. "I have never been married or even courted, so I cannot say with any great amount of certainty, but no, it does not seem wrong. However, the colonel behaves as a proper gentleman should."

"But so did Mr. Wickham when we first met."

Mary shook her head. "No, he spoke too freely about private things to be considered proper."

"But Elizabeth did not seem to think him bad," Lydia protested.

"I dare say Jane did," Mary countered. "And I know that I questioned his actions."

Lydia arched a brow. "And you did not think to mention such a thing to me?"

Mary rolled her eyes. "Would you have listened?"

"Most likely not." Lydia scowled.

Of course, that was only part of the reason. "I also did not think he posed a threat to you other than to make you look foolishly flirtatious."

Lydia's scowl deepened.

"You did like to flirt with handsome gentlemen." Mary gave her sister a pointed look, which caused Lydia to roll her eyes.

"There is nothing wrong with flirting."

"Maybe not in small amounts and quietly."

"I do not wish to argue about flirting," Lydia said with a pout. "I am done with such things, and you have to admit that flirting did help me find a perfectly wonderful gentleman who wishes to marry me."

Mary could not disagree. Lydia, the one sister whom Mary thought would bring shame upon the whole family, had found a respectable gentleman and had managed to become very nearly proper.

"Perhaps I should learn to flirt – but only with gentlemen who call on Mr. Darcy," Mary said with a half-smile. "I truly do not wish to be spinster." She raised a brow at Lydia. "Nor do I wish to marry a parson, unless, of course, he is far better looking and less ridiculous than our cousin."

Lydia laughed. "But I thought you fancied Mr. Collins when he arrived."

"I will admit that I saw him as a way to do something Mama would crow about." She smiled sheepishly at Lydia. "I am dreadful am I not? Wishing to harm gentlemen who do not treat my sisters with respect and contemplating marrying just to finally hear Mama praise me?" She shrugged.

Lydia threw her arms around Mary and pulled her into a tight hug. "Oh, Mary! Being alone in the middle must be dreadful! How you must suffer for it. I will not allow it to be any longer," she said, and then, she did something she had not done since they were both very young. She kissed Mary's cheek.

"We will find you an appropriate husband," she added as she released Mary. "Do you truly not think it is either Lord Westonbury or Mr. Langley? They are both handsome and marrying a viscount would certainly give Mama something to praise." She grasped Mary's shoulders and tipped her head as a very serious expression settled on her face. "People can change. I have. Perhaps even Lord Westonbury could."

Mary shook her head. "I am not certain that such a thing is possible."

"Oh, it is. I am almost certain," Lydia declared. "Why look at Mr. Boxall. He was a dreadful bore and had such wild hair that stood out in every direction whenever he removed his hat. But then, he went to college and came back a bit more inter-esting, though still not entirely free of dullness — but he does read poetry very well — and his hair is nearly always nicely styled now. I would say his wife is a very happy and fortunate creature to have him."

And this was the sister who had pledged herself to help Mary secure a husband? Such rambling thoughts! Mary chuckled. With the amount of exuberance her youngest sister possessed, perhaps Lydia might just succeed. However...

"I think it might take more than a few lessons in elocution and a good barber to make Lord Weston-bury into an acceptable gentleman."

Chapter 8

"Oh, Mr. Darcy!"

Wes opened one eye and peeked at the door to his room which was partially open. Was that Darcy at the door?

"Good day, Miss Lydia. How might I be of service?"

Apparently, Darcy was at the door. Wes groaned and rubbed his aching head. Two days in bed and the blasted thing still hurt – despite his mother's best attempts to do him in with potions from the apothecary.

"I was wondering if you had any friends."

Wes chuckled at Miss Lydia's inquiry. He'd give anything to see Darcy attempt to not look offended at such a comment.

"I have a few," Darcy answered. "Why do you ask?"

"It's for Mary."

Wes strained to hear the words as Lydia's voice had softened. Why did Mary wish to know if Darcy had friends?

"You see, she would like to marry someday."

"That seems reasonable," Darcy inserted.

"And she would like to marry someone who is proper – respectful was the word she used most often."

"I see."

"And I thought that, since the colonel and you were such good friends and both of you are very respectful to ladies, and since you are friends with Mr. Bingley, who also seems very respectful, and since you did such a good job of selecting Sir Matthew for Miss Bingley, you might be an excellent source for names of gentlemen to whom Mary could be introduced."

Mary was searching for a husband in earnest? Wes rubbed his head once again. He wished her well in finding someone who met her exacting standards.

"I am certain my aunt would know of gentlemen who would be excellent choices."

"Oh, we have spoken of it, and she agreed that

asking you would be a good idea. Then, she can add those names to the list she is compiling."

"And Mary knows of this?"

Wes huffed in frustration as there was no audible answer made to Darcy's inquiry.

"Do you mind if I give this some thought?"

She must have answered yes if Darcy was going to think about adding to this list of suitors for Mary.

"We are anxious to begin, but we do not wish to rush things either."

"I thought Mary was out with a potential suitor at present."

"Well..."

Lydia's voice softened again.

"He might not suit. There is a possible smudge on his character, I am afraid."

"Ah, I see," Darcy answered.

What did he see? As far as Wes was concerned there was nothing to see. Very little had been said. What was this smudge of which Lydia spoke? How could one see anything without knowing that detail?

"How is Richard today?"

"He is doing quite well. He read for a full half-hour this morning before his head began to hurt, and he rarely falters at all when he walks. I think he is becoming accustomed to the lack of vision. Shall I send him to you?"

"I would welcome his company if Wes does."

"Why would he not? It is a pleasant thing to know that people care for your wellbeing when you are ill. I will send him to you before I return to my sisters."

"I thank you."

Darcy was still chuckling when he stepped into the room.

"Who has taken Mary out?"

"Good day to you, too," Darcy replied. "I am not entirely certain, but I expect either my wife or one of my sisters will tell me later, especially as I intend to inquire about what seems to be a project to see Mary wed."

"Yes, yes, I would like to know about that as well." Wes pushed up on his pillows. "I think I shall be well enough to be allowed to return to the house on Brook Street tomorrow." His cousin looked absolutely at ease and excessively happy as he lounged in a chair near the bed. "Marriage suits you."

"Yes, it does," Darcy agreed with a grin. "I suggest you try it."

Wes shook his head.

"A simple no? Nothing else? Are you not going to tell me how marriage would encroach upon your freedoms as you normally do?"

"I am ill."

Darcy chuckled. "You are, but you are nearly well enough to leave the safety of Matlock House."

"Yes, well, be that as it may, I am not well enough to formulate a witty rejoinder." And truth be told, he was not certain that he could even if he was completely well. His views of marriage had shifted during his stay in Hertfordshire.

"Ah! You are awake and seemingly alert," Richard said as he entered the room. "Darcy, it is good to see you. I have been instructed that I am also to make an appearance in the sitting room to see your wife, as well as Georgiana and Kitty. However, now is not a good time, as the ladies have much to discuss over tea." He took a seat in a chair Darcy had pulled over next to his. "I can move furniture now without tipping over," he muttered.

"Just allow me to do you this small service so I

can say I did so if questioned later by either my wife or Lydia."

Wes chuckled. "What stratagems are being planned?"

"It is a campaign to see Mary secure a husband. Apparently, she is not intent upon being a spinster, which, from what I hear, has been declared by her mother a time or two. However, Lydia has decided that she should lend her services. Therefore, we are all hopeful for success."

"I had gathered that from the way she was questioning Darcy before he entered the room."

"She was questioning you?" Richard asked Darcy, who nodded.

"She seems to think that if someone is a friend of mine, they will be a respectable sort of fellow."

"It is a good deduction," Richard agreed.

"I am your friend, and I would venture a guess that Miss Mary would not consider me respectable." Wes scowled. There was no need to guess, he knew she did not think of him as anything near respectable.

"This is true," Darcy muttered.

"Mother is quite pleased to have a project such

as this to keep her occupied, and I think it has raised Lydia even more in her eyes."

Darcy laughed.

"At least, if she is occupied with Miss Mary, she might leave me be," Wes said. "Did you both have to find ladies at the same time? Could you not have spread it out a bit?"

Again, Darcy laughed, and Richard joined him.

"It was not planned," Richard said.

"Which is how it should be," Wes said. "Matches should not be forced."

"Miss Bingley's was, and that has worked out quite well," Richard argued.

"That is an exception."

"I am not so certain it is. There are many who have married as arranged and found themselves quite happy," Darcy said.

"And an even greater number have found themselves tied to a life of misery. Have Miss Lydia and our mother considered that?"

"I see the foul mood which led to your riding in the rain and catching a fever has not lifted," Darcy said.

How could it have lifted? Mary thought him as bad as Wickham and was entertaining other suitors. And all of that disturbed him greatly for reasons he was not willing to admit – even to himself.

"I am ill. One is not required to be cheerful when one is ill."

"Duly noted. Wes is not to be expected to formulate witty rejoinders or be pleasant if he is ill." Darcy's lips quirked up into a teasing smile.

"I retract my statement from before. Marriage does not suit you. It has made you unbearably insolent."

Darcy chuckled. "I apologize. I should be more considerate of your indisposition."

"Yes, you should," Wes agreed.

"In all seriousness, how are you?"

"As I said, I will be well enough to return to Brook Street tomorrow, and then I would expect to be laid low for only a day or two longer before I am my formerly witty and charming self."

"I am pleased to hear it," Darcy assured him. "When you are well, my wife would be happy to have you call on us."

The goofy grin Darcy wore every time he mentioned his wife was enviable for it was such a look of complete satisfaction and good fortune.

Darcy shifted his attention to Richard. "I have

already received a report about how you are feeling. Lydia seems pleased with your improvement. I do hope you and she will call on us at Darcy House soon. It has been far too long since you barged into my study."

"Indeed, it has, though I shall do my best to remember to knock now that you have a wife." Richard winked at Darcy, who only grinned once again and assure him that it might be best.

"Have you and your father discussed much about your future yet?" Darcy asked.

"Extensively. He has spoken to a few friends about possible postings that would rely on my mind for strategy and not my physical ability to lead a battalion. However, it does not look promising, and he thinks it would be best if I prepare myself to take up the running of Beaumont Abbey."

Surprisingly, Richard did not look displeased by such a thing.

"And financially?" Darcy asked. "Will that provide what you need?"

Richard nodded. "And it can always be improved. Father has promised a few pounds to help fund some renovations since he thinks Lydia will wish to do some redecorating and there are things which could use modernizing or improving before they fail and cause damage such as the roof on one of the outbuildings."

"I am not opposed to adding to the happiness of a cousin or my wife's sister."

"I know, and I thank you for the offer."

Wes waited for the *however* which would precede a refusal of assistance. Richard had always in the past been adamant that he would make his own way in the world and would not rely on the charity of his relations. Wes waited, but the *however* never came.

"You are accepting his offer?" Wes could not keep the shock from his voice.

"I am. There may be a need for assistance."

"Just like that?" What had become of his brother?

Richard nodded. "I am of no use to the military at present, and I will have a wife for whom to provide. I cannot afford to be cavalier."

"And if I offered to assist you?"

"I would accept it if needed, just as I am doing with Father and Darcy." He blew out a breath. "It is not easily done, I assure you, but I have little choice. This is not just about me any longer. I cannot afford to think only of what I wish. I must put Lydia and whatever family we might have before myself."

"And you will not regret doing so?" Wes asked.

Richard shook his head. "I would regret doing anything which separated me from Lydia or anything which would cause her discomfort or pain. I simply could not bear that."

Wes's eyebrows rose while Darcy nodded as if he completely understood such reasoning.

Richard leaned forward and placed a hand on Wes's. "Loving Lydia and being loved by her in return is the treasure."

"And worth securing and protecting at all costs," Darcy agreed.

Wes's brow furrowed as he considered what it might be like to feel so about someone. His eyes drifted to the door while his mind wandered down the hall and to the sitting room where Mary's future was being discussed, and finally, and with great reluctance, he admitted to himself what he had known since shortly after he had arrived in Hertfordshire. He knew what it felt like to feel as if the love of a particular lady was a prize to be sought, and he knew what it was to long for such a treasure. Unfortunately, he also knew what it was to know that such a treasure would never be his for the lady he desired held him in the greatest contempt.

"I will have to take your word for it," he said.

For he would surely never be so fortunate to be loved as either his brother or Darcy was.

Chapter 9

"You are not leaving." Lord Matlock stood just inside Wes's door the following morning, blocking Wes's path. "Your horse has been returned to the stable. Your mother will not be persuaded to let you leave until you are completely well, and I will not be persuaded to go against her in this."

Wes sat down on the edge of his bed. His father was actually forbidding him from leaving Matlock House? That was new. He had expected his mother to be put out with him for leaving before she declared he was well enough to do so but not his father.

In fact, he had hoped his mother would be put out with him for he was not at all pleased with her at the moment. Mary would not have been out riding in the park with Langley twice already if it had not been for his mother and that completely beguiling pink dress she had insisted Mary wear to that musicale.

He scowled both because he was being forced to do as his mother wished and because apparently, the fact that Langley was familiar with Sally did not make him a completely unsuitable candidate for marriage for Miss Mary.

"I realize," his father continued in a cautious tone, "that you cannot be forced to remain here. You are free to do as you please to a point. However, I would caution you to remember how dearly your mother loves you."

Guilt. That was to be the prison guard, was it?

"You know, of course, that every servant in the house has been instructed not to aid you in departing."

Of course, his mother was proficient at setting a firm line of defense. It really was no wonder his brother had done so well in the military if he had inherited even a fraction of the skills of strategy his mother possessed.

"Therefore," his father continued, "you will have to make your horse ready yourself, as well as pack your things and see to their transport."

"I have servants to see to such things." Had his mother forgotten that fact?

His father grimaced. "Your mother can be demanding."

A sense of foreboding settled in Wes's stomach. "What has she done?"

"Your servants have returned to Brook Street."

Apparently, she had not forgotten about his servants. "She dismissed my servants from the house?" he asked incredulously.

His father nodded.

"And you allowed her to do this?"

His father smiled. "I did not disallow her to do it." He shrugged. "I suppose the two are nearly the same."

"They are exactly the same!"

"Yes, well, be that as it may, I saw Langley after his call yesterday, and I thought it best if you were to remain here for a day or two."

Wes tipped his head, which was once again beginning to ache, and studied his father. "What do you mean?"

Lord Matlock crossed to take a seat near Wes's bed. "There is no need for you to be out of bed."

"I am tired of being in bed," Wes grumbled as he

climbed back onto his bed and settled into his pillows. There was no point in being out of bed if he
had no man to help him dress. "Now, tell me what
you mean."

"Are you not going to remove your robe and slippers?"

"No." Wes folded his arms and waited for his
father to tell him what he wished to know. He had
still not decided if he was going to do as his mother
wished or attempt the feat of getting himself from
his bed here to his bed in Brook Street.

His father chuckled. "You look very much like
you did when you were six, and I refused to allow
you to go see the new lambs because you were still
speckled and itching with chickenpox. You have
never been very good at not getting what you
want." He shook his head. "The silent tantrums
with which your nurses had to deal! I likely should
have paid them more than I did. The sulking and
stewing you would do!" He chuckled again. "Much
like you are doing right now."

He was not sulking and stewing — not really. He
was ill and wished to be away from where he would
hear of Miss Mary and her suitors. Added to that,
the fact that he was being prevented from doing

what he wished was frustrating, and one could be excused for being out of sorts when one was ill. So, therefore, it was different than sulking and stewing. Sort of.

"Does this have anything to do with why I should be here rather than at home?" Wes smoothed the flap of his robe over his legs. There was no sense in being cold due to a refusal to properly tuck himself into bed.

His father nodded and then settled back into his chair, affecting the posture he always took when about to lecture his son on something – elbows propped on the arms of the chair and hands clasped with two fingers steepled upon which he rested his chin. He drew and released a deep breath, and Wes knew that he was indeed going to be lectured about something – though he could not for the life of him think of what it was until his father asked...

"How did Miss Mary know that Langley has visited a brothel?"

"How do you know she knows that?" Wes countered warily. His father rarely asked random questions.

"As I said, I saw Langley before he left yesterday

and bore a great deal of his displeasure on your behalf." His left eyebrow arched. "Did you tell Miss Mary about Langley visiting Sally's?"

"I might have," Wes admitted reluctantly.

"Well, according to what Miss Mary told Langley, you most certainly told her about Sally's."

"If you already knew that, then why did you ask me?"

"I want to know why you told her." He shifted so that his hands were draped over the ends of the chair's arms and his ankles were crossed in front of him. "And do not concoct some story about wishing to see to her wellbeing or some such drivel."

"What if it is not drivel?"

His father shook his head. "It is."

His father seemed entirely too confident and relaxed.

"Then, what do you think is my reason?" Wes retorted. "You appear to suspect an answer."

"Are you certain you wish me to answer that?" The right side of his father's lips lifted in a half-smile.

"I think I should like to hear your suppositions." And truly, he was curious to hear them, despite the niggly fear that told him to not press for the answer. He should likely just be happy that Langley had been sent packing and leave it at that.

"You are smitten with her. I saw it in how you watched her at Netherfield."

"I am not." Wes's ears grew warm at the lie.

"You are, and jealousy made you tell her about Langley's shortcomings."

Wes had always admired his father's insight and wisdom until this moment. He turned his eyes away from his father and looked at the wall across from his bed. "If you are correct, and I am not saying you are, it matters very little. Miss Mary thinks of me as no better than Wickham."

"I beg your pardon?" His father's tone was incredulous.

"She thinks I am no better than Wickham."

"Why?"

Wes blew out a breath. "I asked her sisters for a kiss one night when I was well into my cups and leaving Sally's. I thought they were..." What? Prostitutes? Light skirts? Women of the night? He could not bring himself to call either Lydia or Elizabeth such a thing even if it was what he had thought at the time. "Well, they were at Sally's."

"Ah, yes. Your mother told me about that. So

how does that relate to you being thought of as a scoundrel by Miss Mary?"

If he only knew the answer to that!

"I am certain I could not say. However, she has accused me of taking advantage of women and was angry at first that I did not know who her sisters were when I asked them for a kiss and then when she asked if I knew anything about the women at Sally's and I told her I did, she became even more furious and said..." He paused mid-ramble as a thought pricked his aching brain.

What had Lydia said to Darcy yesterday? Mary wished for a gentleman who was proper and respectful. And she had accused him of treating her sisters ill. Understanding dawned with a putrid sickening feeling.

"She thinks I am incapable of respecting her." He shook his head. "Wickham seeks only to please himself." The words hit him as soundly as a punch from his sparring partner at Gentleman Jacksons would, but they hurt far more. "In Mary's eyes, I am a self-centered bounder."

"And what do you think?" his father asked.

"I do not think I am. Do you?" He looked to his father for an answer.

"What I think does not signify."

"But it does. What if she is right and I am wrong?" The horror of such at thing gripped his chest, squeezing the air from his lung so that he could only breath in quick, shallow breaths.

His father leaned forward. "If you are not what she says, then prove it to her, and if, after some soul searching, you find you are what she claims you are, then change your ways. *You* must decide who *you* are going to be."

How many times had his father said something very similar to that to him?

You are the one who decides who you become, Son. Not some title, not your friends, not even your mother can make that decision for you. Your future is yours alone.

And he had taken that advice and had only used it to justify pleasing himself while ignoring its deeper meaning. How foolish he had been!

"How do I do that? How do I prove myself to her?"

"Only you can decide, my son."

"That is far from helpful," Wes grumbled.

His father shook his head. "You are wrong. My solving your problem will not help you as much as your figuring out the solution on your own will." He reached over and patted Wes's leg. "If you love Miss Mary, as I suspect you do, the toil will be worth the reward." He pushed up from his chair and crossed to the door.

"But what if I cannot do it?" Something very akin to panic settled upon Wes's shoulders and began stirring his emotions.

"My lord, Reginald Arthur Fitzwilliam, Viscount Westonbury, the first-born and heir of the body of Lord Matlock, incapable of obtaining that for which he wishes?" His father's smile reached all the way to his eyes. "Not possible, unless he is far less like his mother than I suppose and not at all the man I know him to be." And with those parting words, his father ducked out the door, leaving Wes to ponder the problem named Miss Mary on his own.

Chapter 10

No sooner had Mary's feet both landed in the library than she wanted them to take her out of the room, for she was completely unprepared to see Lord Westonbury sitting at the desk, writing. She had thought him still confined to his room.

"Wait just a moment. I am nearly finished," he called to her before she could make her escape. "I should like to return your book to you before you run away."

"I was not –" Mary pressed her lips together. She was running away. There was no use in denying it. Silently, she perched on the edge of a chair near the door.

He looked up at her. "I have not read the entire thing."

She nodded. She was surprised that he had read any of it. She leaned forward so she could see better what he was doing. Was he copying from the book?

He placed his pen in its holder and closed the book in front of him. Turning in his chair, he extended the book to her.

He had been copying from it! How peculiar.

"I only got as far as the Preliminary Observations. I have not been home to read, you see. I only had the book brought over today."

She rose and crossed to him to claim her book. "You may keep it longer if you wish."

Her offer was met with a shake of his head. "I did page through it and read a few snatches here and there, but if I am to be honest with you — and I would never be anything less..."

The brow over her left eye arched as he placed his hand on his heart and held her gaze.

"Never," he repeated.

Her brow furrowed. What was he playing at?

He sighed. "As I was saying, if I were to be honest, there is a great deal of information in that book which appears to be excessively boring." He smiled. "I knew it was not easy to be a female, but I did not realize it was so tediously demanding. What you wear, how you walk, what colour looks best, what style, how your hair is coiffeured, your deportment." He shook his head. "It is a wonder that all ladies do not retire to the country and live in seclusion to avoid being held to such exacting standards."

"The standards do not disappear just because one changes location," Mary retorted. "Any lady who respects herself will hold herself to a standard of excellence wherever she is." She would do well to remember that and refrain from being shrewish even if someone deserved admonishment.

"Ah! Yes!" He picked up his page. "'*Reverence thyself,' says the philosopher, not only with relation to the mind which directs, but to the body which executes.*'"

Mary peered at the paper from which he read. There were several scrawled notes on it.

"There were some good things in what I read which I did not wish to forget," he explained.

There were things he did not wish to forget? From her book? A book written to ladies? That was curious. "What else have you written?"

He shook his head, pulling the paper back from her searching eyes. "No, first, did I use the right quote?"

He looked at her with such hopeful expectation

— as if her opinion was the most important one in the whole world. And once again, though she smiled at him, she wondered what he was about.

"Yes, that was a perfect quote. But can you explain it?"

Amusement flickered in his eyes and played at his smirk. "Are you practising to be a governess?"

"No, I would be a dreadful governess. I do not have the patience for it. Now, kindly explain the meaning of what you have quoted. It does very little good to memorize something and not understand it."

"I think you would make a very good governess with comments such as that." His chuckle as he stood was interrupted by a cough before he could walk from where he was to a chair nearer the hearth in which a small fire was burning. "Join me," he said, motioning to a chair that stood next to his but with a table between them.

Mary considered refusing only for a moment before she joined him as he placed his feet on a stool and tipped his head back against the wing of his chair.

"Are you certain you should be out of bed?" she asked as she arranged her skirts. Between his coughing and now his look of exhaustion, she doubted it.

"Yes, but not for any noble reason." He smirked. "I am defying my mother. It is a most dreadful thing to admit, I know, but I was not pleased to be told I could not return to my home in Brook Street. And so, I am attempting to convince her that I am well enough."

"But you are not."

He sighed. "So, I am discovering. Writing a few lines on a bit of paper should not weary one as much as it has me. However, I suppose tiredness and a slightly aching head is the just punishment for being so obstinate."

"So I have been told." More than once by her mother when she had become indisposed due to following her own way instead of heeding Jane's advice.

"Do we share a trait?"

Mary nodded. "Not a good one, I am afraid."

He chuckled. "And not a bad one either, or so my mother informs me. Persistence and determination are excellent things when they are properly directed."

That was true, and she reluctantly admitted so

to him while she wondered if his obstinacy could indeed be directed in some fashion as to be beneficial to someone other than himself and his desires.

"Now, to my explanation," he said. "From what I have read, which admittedly is not much, one must not prefer the mind over the body or the body over the mind. They should be equally respected for it is the body which executes the power and substance of the mind. Therefore, how one presents her or himself to the world is a representation of what flows in the mind, and behaviour, as well as dress, is, in that way, an indicator of the character of a person and his or her virtue or lack thereof." He held up a finger. "Or it could be an indicator of his or her lack of respect for the protection of said virtue."

That was impressively accurate. It seemed his lordship was not beyond pondering things of substance.

"That is why you have rightly accused me of being what I thought I was not," he added.

Mary's cheeks burned with shame. "I must apologize for my lack of restraint in speaking." How did such a lack of restraint reflect upon her character? Not well, she feared.

He shook his head. "Do not be sorry for it. I believe it was what I needed to hear."

"I still should not have said it."

He shrugged. "Perhaps. However, your passion for what is virtuous is commendable, even if it stung to hear it."

Her heart pinched. She had wanted to slap him with her words — desired it with all her heart even — but the resounding painful thwack which he had just voiced was not satisfactory at all. There was no feeling of joy for a strike well-placed, nor was there a feeling of justification for her reasons for wishing to strike him.

"I have had time to think between sleeping and sipping broth. I must apologize for how I treated your sisters."

Was that it? He had stopped and was watching her as if he expected her to reply. Was that all he had thought about? Did he not see how his treatment of her sisters was just an indicator of a larger issue?

He shifted uneasily when she did not reply. "I have not thought beyond that, to be honest," he added. "And I will only ever be honest with you. I have made myself that pledge."

"You have?" The thought of him pledging to himself on her behalf was incredulous to her mind while also being... quite pleasing. It was almost as if what she thought mattered and not just in some insignificant way but in a fundamental way. That was likely the heart of the matter and what caused her shock for she had not thought he cared one fig about what she thought other than for it to provide him with fodder with which to provoke her.

He nodded. "I think friendships are best when based on truthfulness. I should very much like to be your friend and, if you will allow me to be such and not scurry away anytime you see me, then I will have the chance to apologize for whatever other shortcomings my musings might reveal."

"Are you certain you wish that? I have proven myself unable to keep from scolding and lecturing." There was something about him which loosened her tongue as nothing else did. Granted, she struggled at the best of times to keep her opinions to herself, but with him, it was a losing battle even before it started.

"I wish it. All of it. Your friendship, your scolding, and your lecturing." His lips tipped up in a very charming smile. "I shall even strive to not behave in such a way as to cause you to scold or lecture, although I cannot promise to succeed. I am a troublesome fellow and have been all my life." He chuckled and then coughed before sobering. "I would beg you to tell me when you see a fault – although it would be most appreciated if it could be done in a gentle fashion."

Mary smiled. No one — absolutely no one — had ever requested for her to scold them. No one had ever even asked her to share her opinion with them. She grimaced. Of course, that could be attributed to the fact that she rarely gave them a moment to request it, tending to rather spew forth her thoughts without invitation. She really did need to read the book she held. The amount of grace she possessed was minimal at best.

"Please, grant me your friendship so that I can prove to you that I am a better man than Wickham."

Her left brow once again arched skeptically.

"I have not been to Sally's since before I arrived in Hertfordshire."

She had not expected him to share such information with her. It was startling and caused her cheeks to flush.

"I know it is not proper to discuss such things," he said before she could inform him that he should not be sharing such things with her.

"However, since you know that I have visited there and you have equated that with me being like Wickham, I thought it important for you to know that bit of information."

Again, he was looking at her as if what she thought was of utmost importance. Yet, she still wondered if this all could just be a game to him.

"How long will you abstain from such things?" She looked at her hands, for there was no way she could look at him and be so direct. As it was, her heart was drumming a rapid pace and her cheeks, which had been merely warm, were now burning. Be that as it may, she needed to hear his response to such an improper question so that she could judge whether or not his pledge to himself, regarding being honest with her, was real or a façade put in place to sway her opinion.

"It may surprise you to know I have thought that very question."

She dared to peek up at him. That did surprise her.

"And I have no answer, for presently, I do not

know. I should like to say forever, but I feel that to promise such at this moment would be unwise as it is early days."

If it had surprised Mary that he had questioned himself about how long he might abstain from visiting a brothel, his answer to that very question utterly shocked her. Only a gentleman who was being abjectly honest with her would admit to not knowing, while a gentleman who was merely playing at being honest would have replied forever without a second thought. Perhaps she could trust him enough to grant him what he desired.

She tipped her head and studied him. There appeared to be no mask to his appearance. Trepidation shone in his eyes. Had they always been that lovely shade of blue?

His bottom lip was just slightly drawn in as if he might be holding the back of it between his teeth. He needed a shave for his jaw was speckled with whiskers.

"Are you doing this only because of what I said about Wickham?"

One shoulder lifted and lowered and then he shook his head. "That is only part of it – a great part of it, I would suppose. How could I not wish to prove myself unlike a man as disreputable as Wickham? But, you will remember that I said I have not visited Sally's since before I arrived in Hertfordshire."

She nodded. He had said that.

"This is not easily admitted, and I have not said a word of this to anyone else."

"I will not repeat it," she assured him.

"There are two reasons for my failure to return to Sally's. The first is that I have seen my cousin and brother happy in a way I have never been, which would seem to many to have very little to do with visiting a brothel, but to my mind it does. Theirs is not a fleeting satisfaction." Again, he shrugged.

"And the other reason?" The less time they could spend on discussing lasting and fleeting satisfaction, the better.

"You disapprove of it." He gave her a sheepish smirk. "Not even my mother's disapproval has kept me from Sally's. Of course, that is likely because I know that even when she locks me out of the house, I will still have her love. However, you are not required by familial relations to tolerate me or extend me your friendship."

"And you wish for my good opinion so much?"

"Disturbing, is it not?"

"Unsettling," she admitted. It was unsettling to the point of causing her heart to flutter at the thought.

"So what do you say? May I be so fortunate as to gain your tentative acceptance as a friend?" He folded his hands and gave her a beseeching look. "Please?"

Her left brow arched over her eye once again. She was still not entirely certain he was not playing at some scheme, but he had proven himself somewhat worthy of, at least, consideration.

"Yes, tentatively," she replied. She had endured her youngest sister for fifteen years – and Lydia was a troublesome sister – surely, she could also tolerate yet another trying relation.

Chapter 11

People moved slowly from door to ballroom and then circled the perimeter of the room. A few matrons, well past their prime, dragged their charges to chairs at the far end where they sat and whispered behind fans to the poor young things left to their care.

Much to Wes's amusement, one young lady with brown hair and a lovely smattering of freckles across her nose pulled herself straight and affixed a smile after such a whispered conversation. He continued to watch her as she rolled her eyes heavenward before closing them. Whomever the fussing old woman behind the large blue fan was, it was obvious to Wes that her idea of how a lady must present herself and how the young lady thought she should present herself were completely different. He might seek an introduction later if she continued to be entertaining. That should puff her guardian up quite well. He stumbled forward, his observation of the young woman interrupted by someone carelessly wading through the crowd.

"You were not home earlier, Westonbury."

Tension clamped down between Wes's shoulders. "Langley. It is good to see you." It wasn't really, but that was not the thing to say in a ballroom, especially to someone who was scowling as his friend was.

"I had wished to have a chat with you."

"A chat you say?" Wes replied as nonchalantly as he could. He highly doubted it was a chat for which Langley wished. The man had, after all, not been happy the last time he had been at Matlock House.

"We will call it that, although an invitation to Gentleman Jackson's might be more accurate." Langley straightened his sleeve. "Accosting a scoundrel in his home is frowned upon."

"That young woman across the way. The one next to the silver-haired matron with the blue fan. She's pretty, is she not?"

"Do not attempt to change the subject," Langley grumbled but then added, "Yes, I do believe she is. I've never seen her before."

"You should seek an introduction. I had thought to, but I have duties to perform tonight before I am allowed to sneak back to my bed. My blasted head keeps hurting."

"Are you still unwell?"

"Enough to not be allowed to return home to Brook Street," Wes answered. "Though I do think I might be freed after tonight if I can play the part of happy soiree attendee."

"I have half a mind to go tell your mother you have a headache and coughed three times," Langley retorted.

"If you must."

Langley's eyes narrowed. "Well, I am not going to if that is what you wish."

"Then, do not tell her."

Langley huffed. "I wish for once you were not so sneaky as you are, for I would dearly like to know whether you wished to stay at Matlock House or not so that I could interfere with your desires as you have with mine."

"Yes, about that," Wes allowed his eyes to scan the room as if he was speaking of nothing of great significance, "I must apologize. It was shabby of me to tell Miss Mary of ... well, I am certain I do not need to say it here where others might hear."

"Shabby does not describe it by half!"

Wes shrugged. "Gentleman Jackson's, you say?"

Langley's mouth dropped open for a moment. "Not when you are ill." He leaned closer and whispered. "Your mother terrifies me at times. I should not like to be the cause of her ill son becoming more ill."

"Billiards then? Or cards? You could fleece me."

Langley chuckled and shook his head. "No, I could not, and you know it."

"If I allowed it, you could."

"Yes, being allowed to trounce you would make me feel so vindicated."

Wes chuckled at his friend's sardonic tone. "You realize that I would have to allow you to trounce me at Jackson's, too, do you not?"

"Not necessarily. There is a greater chance I can best you at boxing than at cards or billiards." He sighed. "You know I do not visit... there... as you do. Twice. I have been there twice." He shook his head. "And both times at your suggestion."

It had been a week since Mary had accused him of being like Wickham, but Langley's words reminded him perfectly of the pain of being found wanting by someone for whom you cared – even if that someone was not a pretty but stern and proper young miss but rather one's best friend of many years.

"Which is why I wish to allow you to trounce me. I deserve it."

People pushed past them, causing them to step back to allow for the movement.

"You do?" Langley whispered.

Wes nodded. "It was shabby of me to do as I did."

"Then why did you? You had already said that you were not going to pursue her."

Wes shook his head. "No, I believe I said I was not going to seduce her."

Confusion suffused his friend's face. "Are they not the same thing to you?"

Again, Wes shook his head. Not anymore. He was about to move from where he stood to go greet the Bennet ladies and Darcy until a thought stopped him. He turned to his friend. "Were you pursuing her to seduce her?" He took several quick and not as calming as he had hoped breaths. "For if you were, I take it back and am not sorry in the least for having interfered."

Langley held up his hands in defense. "No. Remember, I know your mother."

"Then why were you pursuing her?" Wes demanded.

"To see if we would suit. She is pretty and seems interesting, and your mother approves of her, so it would stand to reason she might be a good match."

Well, that was not as comforting as he wished it was. The idea of Mary and Langley still caused a thick, dark cloud to settle over him. "Come. I will introduce you to her sister."

Langley grabbed his elbow. "Wait. You still have not answered me. Why did you do what you did?"

"Not here," Wes said.

Langley folded his arms and moved not an inch to follow him.

Wes sighed.

"Very well. Jealousy." And with that, he turned and walked away. If Langley wished to meet Mary's sister, he could catch up and if not, he could just stay there, looking astonished.

"You cannot always have what you wish," Langley hissed when he had finally caught up to Wes.

"No, I suppose not." He turned away from Langley. "Darcy, Mrs. Darcy, Miss Kitty," he greeted.

"I am happy to see you are better," Elizabeth said.

"Almost better," Langley muttered, causing Elizabeth's brow to arch suspiciously – much, Wes noticed, like Mary's did when she did not believe him.

"My mother is making a few introductions for Miss Bennet and Miss Lydia. I am certain she will greet you as soon as she knows you are here."

"How is the colonel?" Kitty asked.

"He is here. In the card room, at present. Father will take him home if needed." Wes smiled. "But, not until he has either taken a turn of the ballroom or danced with Miss Lydia." He glanced over his shoulder. "Mrs. Darcy, have you met my friend?"

"Yes, I have. At Matlock House"

"And you, Miss Kitty? May I introduce you to my friend?"

Darcy nodded when Kitty looked his direction.

"Miss Kitty, this is Mr. Langley. Langley, Miss Kitty, sister to Miss Lydia, Miss Bennet, and Mrs. Darcy."

"Mr. Langley who took Mary driving?" Kitty whispered.

"Yes, but I may have painted him as worse than he is," Wes whispered in return. "He is actually a relatively decent fellow. Safe enough for a young lady such as yourself to dance with." As long as the young lady was not Mary.

"The trials I bear by being Westonbury's friend," Langley said lightly while shooting a very displeased look at Wes.

"I am rather troublesome," Wes agreed.

"Indeed," Darcy muttered. "I have not heard too much against you, Mr. Langley."

"It is good to know I am not entirely ruined." Again, Langley's tone was light, but his glare was anything but.

Oh, his foul mood had caused a rather tenuous situation for his friend. Wes had not considered how what he had said about Sally's would affect Langley any further than it would likely separate him from Mary. He was a cad, for who but a cad would treat his friend in such a fashion?

"Would you be willing to give my friend a chance to prove himself better than I have portrayed him to be by allowing him to claim a dance?" Wes leaned forward. "I am asking so that you may freely refuse without being forced to sit out the whole night. I will relay your wishes to him."

Kitty giggled. "I think he can hear you, my lord."

"Pretend he cannot."

She giggled a second time and while wearing a delightfully impertinent look, she said, "I would be happy to dance with your friend, and I would even accept a dance from you as well, my lord."

"That is excellent news since my mother would be displeased if she thought I had not done my duty to see you with at least one partner tonight."

"Then, you have done better than your duty, if your friend asks me."

She was a teasing one. So different from Mary. More like a standard debutante but perhaps a trifle sweeter and more naïve. She had not been in town long enough for the ton to harden her. Strangely, that thought pricked his heart. Though he had not known her long, he would hate to see Miss Kitty changed from the girl he knew.

"I would be honored if you would allow me a set of dances." Langley shot Wes a glance. "Perhaps the first?"

Wes did not care if his friend did take the first

set. He was hoping to secure someone else for those dances.

A grin spread across Miss Kitty's face as she eagerly accepted.

"And might I have the second set?" Wes asked.

"Oh, good. You have done as you should." Lady Matlock breezed up to Wes with Lydia and Mary just behind her. "Did he not offer you the first set?" she inquired of Kitty.

"It was already taken," Wes inserted. "Langley has received that honor."

"Which means you are free!" She looked at her charges. "Miss Mary, I think it must be you who claims Reginald's first set." She leaned toward Mary. "I saw Mrs. Salter."

The comment seemed strange to Wes. Why would it matter if Mrs. Salter was here or not? Although he was happy to hear the information so he could steer clear of that woman and her daughter.

"But what of Lydia?" Mary asked.

Was she attempting to avoid him or was she truly concerned for her sister?

"Richard wishes to stand up with her for that set. He thought it best to make his attempt before the night drew on." Lady Matlock looked at Wes. "Stay near him. It will not be easy."

"That goes without saying," Wes assured her. He had intended to make certain that his brother's first foray into society was as easy as could be. There would be stares. It was to be expected – both because of his scar, which was still fresh-looking, and because he, the colonel who dodged every father and mother's attempt to attach him to their daughter, was attached to a lady few knew. "We could wait for him at the far door if it would be better. Or, we could collect him from the card room?"

"I would think that would be best." His mother motioned for Lydia and Mary to move toward Wes, who offered each an arm. However, before they could leave her, she whispered with some force, "Do not let go of my sons." She gave each girl a pointed look. "I will not have *that* woman attaching herself to either of them. But I would like her to see you – both of you."

To his surprise, Mary smiled first at his mother and then him. "We will do our best to see they are kept safe."

Two chits were to keep him and Richard safe, were they?

"Which woman?" He whispered as they began making their way to the card room.

"My goodness, they are all watching us, are they not?" Lydia whispered.

"And why should they not? You are both pretty, and you are with me."

Mary huffed softly.

"It is true. I tend to draw attention. A viscount in want of a wife and all that. Now, from whom are you protecting me?"

"Mrs. Salter," Lydia whispered. "She is dreadful."

Wes shuddered. "Indeed, she is."

"Yes, and not even you deserve her for a mother-in-law," Mary said quite dryly with what was likely the most bewitching smirk Wes had ever seen.

"Marry me," he whispered to Mary. "And then I shall never have to fear such a terrible fate." He was nearly joking with her.

"I will stay by your side as long as I can to keep you free from scandal, but I am not prepared to do more than that, my lord." She used the same laughing, dry tone from before.

"Are you certain?" He kept his tone light as if his heart was not half-serious.

The hand on his right arm tighten. Glancing down, he saw Lydia looking at him with eyes that were dancing with barely contained excitement. The expression was a bit worrisome while also being annoying since it took his attention away from the Bennet sister he wished to observe.

"I am only tentatively your friend, my lord. Let us leave it at that."

"If you insist," he agreed with a smile, while silently he wondered just how long it might take to convince her to be more.

Chapter 12

"I see Colonel Fitzwilliam has found a pretty little thing to take him on. Poor man, such a devastating blow he received. It is a wonder he has found a lady at all, for as I hear it, his future is rather bleak."

Mrs. Salter sniggered at her companion's words. "Serves the little wench right if you ask me. One should not aspire to such heights when one does not have the pedigree."

Wes, who had only just finished his set of dances with Kitty and was making a tour of the ballroom before taking his leave to find his father and Richard in the card room, took a step closer to Mrs. Salter and the biddy of a woman who had been talking to Mrs. Salter at Almack's when he first heard the name Lydia Bennet.

"And that is precisely why you do not want a second son as a match. Their livelihood is so tenuous." Mrs. Salter lifted her chin and, as she waved her fan in front of her face, surveyed the ballroom with a regal air. "I have pointed out his brother, the viscount, to my Florence." She smirked at her friend. "If that bit of fluff who was on his arm earlier can entice him to dance with her, I see no reason why my Florence cannot do so as well."

Aside from the fact that Miss Salter was not Mary? Well... Wes took out his quizzing glass and pretended to watch the dancing. Miss Salter's most glaring deficit was her mother.

"You are very harsh on them. I have never seen either lady before in my life, and surely could not condemn them on such short notice." Mrs. Salter's friend giggled behind her fan. She was quite obviously not surprised at all by the harshness of her friend nor was she opposed to such behaviour.

"My lord."

Wes turned to see Mary with Kitty standing at her side.

"May I be of service?"

"Your mother wished us to tell you that your brother is likely going to depart, and your father was wondering if you wished to see him home since you have not been feeling well," Kitty explained.

"And my mother could not come tell me this?"

"She is introducing Lydia to someone," Mary explained.

"Why are you not dancing?" Not that he was particularly upset by the fact that Mary was without a partner for this dance.

"Your mother thought it best for us to spend this set with her obtaining introductions," Kitty said. "Then, we are to be matched with Mr. Darcy if there is no success in any other area."

"She is demanding, is she not?" He smiled at his companions and was about to extend an arm to each of them when Mrs. Salter finally spotted him.

"Oh, my, Lord Westonbury." She dipped an exaggerated curtsey.

He looked at her blankly. "Have we met, Madame?"

"Yes, yes, a month or so ago at Almack's."

He arched an eyebrow. They had not been introduced anywhere. She was posturing in an attempt to make him accept the falsehood rather than look impolite. Unfortunately for her, he was in no mood to be thought polite by the likes of her or her friend.

"I do not remember an introduction, so if you will excuse me. I have friends and a brother – how did you refer to him? Oh, yes, the poor man — who requires my assistance."

Mrs. Salter's eyes grew wide and an affronted gasp escaped her. However, she was not easily put off. "I am certain we have met. I would not forget you."

"But I would forget you." His eyes narrowed. "And your daughter."

Again, she gasped, though just lightly. "Not every lady will turn a blind eye to certain behaviours, my lord. However, my daughter knows that sometimes those with great wealth and power favour certain diversions." Her lips curled into a spiteful smirk as her eyes swept Mary. "That being said, she will not stoop to becoming such a diversion without the benefit of a license as some will."

"Do you mean me?" Mary asked in surprise.

"Well, considering your mother..." Mrs. Salter shrugged.

"You overstep." Wes's tone was as deep and dark as the anger he felt at her insult to Mary. If Mrs.

Salter were a gentleman, he'd be seeing her at the end of a pistol at dawn – no matter what the laws said.

However, Mrs. Salter was neither put off easily nor was she excessively intelligent, for instead of making her apologies and being on her way, she flicked her fan and said in a cajoling tone, "Come now, my lord. We all know you already have one mistress, and well, Miss Bennet is rather beneath you. What other purpose could there be in escorting her here and there like a puppet." All this she said while not looking at him at all, but rather while keeping her taunting gaze fixed upon Mary.

He turned to Mary and Kitty. "My apologies," he said with a tight smile.

"For what?" Kitty asked.

"Any scene I might be about to create."

"My lord, please," Mary begged him. "She is not worth a scene."

He held her gaze. "But you are."

Then, he turned to Mrs. Salter who was tittering behind her fan. "Had," he said.

"I beg your pardon?" Mrs. Salter blinked in surprise.

"I *had* a mistress – one, one mistress, never any

other – however, that arrangement is no longer in place, and I am not looking for another – not even if your daughter were to throw herself at me with her skirts around her ears." He took a step closer to the repugnant matron.

"Allow me to clarify the relationship between you and I. There is none. I have not been introduced to you. That was a fabrication you have used to circumvent propriety, which is likely not unusual for one of your ilk. From this hour forward, you will not seek an introduction to me either for yourself or your daughter. If you do, I will refuse the introduction and make certain to cut you in a most public fashion." He lifted his chin and looked down his nose at her.

"Mr. Darcy will be quite displeased to hear how you have spoken of his sisters, and my mother... well..." he shrugged, "neither she nor my father have ever taken kindly to people treating their guests poorly."

"Guests?" her tone was mocking. "How convenient for both you and your brother."

Wes closed his eyes and drew a breath in through his mostly functioning nose as his heart hammered in his ears.

"Madame, you know not of what you speak," he kept his tone flat and measured. "The Miss Bennets are upstanding young ladies of exceptional character and quality. Should your daughter ever manage to raise herself above you to become as lovely as any of the Bennet ladies are, she could do no better than to secure a gentleman such as my brother. I will brook no disparagement of him or my friends."

He turned to Mary and Kitty. "Come. The earl and countess are waiting."

"Oh, that was well done," Kitty whispered.

"Kitty," Mary scolded.

"What?"

Wes glanced at Mary as they made their way out of the ballroom. She opened her mouth as if to answer her sister but then closed it again. Was she displeased by his behaviour? Was this yet another thing for which he would have to atone? Not that it mattered if she disapproved of what he had done. He could not have done less than he did, for he would not see her treated so.

When they were well away from the ballroom door she finally spoke.

"One does not congratulate a gentleman on his

well-spoken and proper defense of oneself or their loved ones until after one has departed the scene with one's head held high."

Again, he glanced at her. She was attempting to look all that was proper, but her lips twitched when she caught his eye.

"Thank you," she whispered just as they reached the card room.

Had two words ever sounded so sweet? He thought not. He longed to tell her that he would defend her to the end of his life if required. However, in light of the fact that she had reminded him that they were only friends earlier that evening, he refrained and accepted her gratitude with a simple nod of his head and a smile.

"Are you leaving us?" he asked Richard.

"I do not want to," his brother replied, "but my head is beginning to spin."

"Do you think a stroll in the garden might be achievable before we depart?" Wes asked.

"You wish to go with me?"

Wes nodded. "Your head is not the only one to be unhappy with its surroundings." He rubbed the spot between his eyes. "I hate to admit this, but hanging my head over a steaming bowl of water would be a welcome relief. However, I cannot leave just yet. We have a point to carry."

"What have I missed?" his mother asked rather eagerly.

"Mrs. Salter," Mary answered.

Lady Matlock's eyebrows rose.

"She insulted both me and Richard, as well as all the Bennets." He blew out a breath. "Miss Kitty or Miss Bennet can tell you all the details later. However, I thought it might make a grand statement about our acceptance of the Miss Bennets if Richard were to take a turn of the garden with Lydia – accompanied by you and father so that woman cannot claim there was some clandestine reason for a tour of the garden, and I could dance the next set with Miss Mary."

"Two sets, my lord? I think not," Mary protested. "There will be speculation. Expectations will be raised where they should not be."

"Then, I will dance with Miss Kitty."

"That would also be two sets," Mary replied.

"It really must be either you or Miss Kitty," Lady Matlock asserted.

Wes's brow furrowed. What was that sly look she shared with Lydia about?

"Do you wish to have your sister be the topic of whispers or yourself?" his mother pressed.

Mary looked as if she was going to be ill. The thought was not exactly comforting. No gentleman wished for the thought of dancing with him to cause such panic in a young lady.

"We made a grand exit. That is likely enough," he offered. "I would never wish to make you uneasy, Miss Mary, just because I wished to stir up jealousy in another. In fact, stirring up jealousy is likely wrong to do."

"It is likely wrong, and yet I cannot say I do not also wish to see her jealous," Mary admitted. "But we are only friends, my lord, and two sets would make people think we are more than that."

"Right." He nodded as if he agreed with her. "I will help you and Miss Kitty find Darcy and then wait near the door for Richard."

"Why not join us in the garden?" Lady Matlock offered.

"No," Wes said. "That might imply more of a friendship than what Miss Bennet feels comfortable with, and I will not make her feel uneasy." Even if it did nothing to assuage his own desires. "Miss Kitty," he offered his arm first to her and then turned to Mary. "I believe this set will be over soon."

"Have I disappointed you?" Mary asked him quietly.

He nodded. "I should like to say no to ease your mind, but I am afraid my oath to always be honest with you cannot allow me to do that."

She smiled sadly at him.

"I am almost certain I can handle a little disappointment," he said lightly. "Though I must say, I am not at all used to accepting it. I am a selfish creature."

He blew out a breath. There was a wrong he needed to right.

"That is why I told you about Mr. Langley and Sally's. You would not accept me as a friend and so I did not wish for you to accept him either. It was badly done, especially when Langley has only ever called at Sally's twice." Oh, this was going to make her dislike him again. He could feel it in the way her hand gripped his arm more firmly. "Both times were because of me. He would not have gone there on his own."

Thankfully, Darcy was approaching them. He would not need to hear her shocked reply, nor would he have to endure her displeasure. It was likely cowardly of him to seek an easy escape, but presently, he did not care to be brave and soldier on. What was there to defend? He should rightly be dismissed and sent away, and that was precisely what he was doing to himself.

"My mother and father have gone to take a turn of the garden with Richard and Miss Lydia before Richard and I take our leave."

"You are leaving?" Darcy asked in surprise. "I thought your father was to take Richard home if he needed to leave."

"I am almost well, but not quite."

"I thank you for attending despite feeling unwell and for helping my sisters and me through this first ball," Elizabeth said with a smile.

"It is what one does for his family and friends." He allowed his eyes to hold Mary's as he said the word friends. Hopefully, after his revelation about Langley, they were still friends. However, her expression was not giving him any indication of where they stood.

"I will leave these ladies with you, Darcy, and say my goodnights. I hope the rest of the ball is even better than the beginning." He gave them a bow and took his leave.

Chapter 13

Mary took her place across from Darcy in the new set which was forming. Lydia had not yet returned from her stroll in the garden, and Kitty was going to keep Elizabeth company while they awaited Lady Matlock's return. A gentleman with sandy brown hair and an easy smile had taken the seat next to Kitty.

"Do you know him?" Mary tipped her head toward her sisters.

Darcy nodded. "Not overly well, but I do know him."

"Has he been introduced to either of my sisters?"

"Not to my knowledge."

Mary's left eyebrow arched. Then, he should not be talking to them. "Do we wish to sit out this dance?"

Darcy's brow furrowed. "It would leave a hole

in the formation, and we are about to begin. However, I will not deny wishing to extricate Mr. Banks from his seat." His shoulders lifted and lowered as he took a deep breath. "My aunt and uncle will return soon."

He sounded almost as if he believed that. But he was correct about them beginning sooner rather than later, for no sooner had Darcy finished speaking and taken one more concerned look toward his wife and Kitty than the musicians began their work.

"There are rules for a reason," Mary grumbled as she joined hands with Darcy.

"I could not agree more."

The dance spun them from one place in the line to another, crossing over and back, and circling around the people next to them. All through the movements of the dance, Mary stewed over the lack of regard for rules that Mr. Banks was so blatantly demonstrating.

She stumbled during one of her turns because she was watching to see how Kitty responded, but thankfully, Darcy caught her arm before she could make a complete fool of herself by falling.

Where were Lord and Lady Matlock? The dance was half over, and they had not yet returned.

"No harm will befall them," Darcy whispered in an almost convincing tone. "Do try to enjoy the dance."

Mary smiled and nodded. There was little danger to be found in a gentleman merely talking to her sisters in a crowded room. It just bothered her to an exasperating level that he was doing so without an introduction. She could more easily forgive such behaviour at an assembly in Meryton as things were not always as proper at those events as she had expected them to be here in town.

"I have never heard anything untoward about him," Darcy added the next time they met.

"I am being foolish, am I not?"

"No, you are not," he assured her. "You, just like me, prize rules and regulations."

They were separated for several steps before joining hands and passing up and down the line of dancers.

"That is commendable," Darcy added.

Was it truly? It seemed to be something which made life much more challenging than it was for those such as Lydia who held onto rules loosely –

or she did. However, now, Mary was not entirely certain how her sister viewed rules. It seemed as if Lydia was more in favour of them than she had ever been.

Was it possible that she, herself, ventured toward the opposite end of the spectrum and held onto rules too firmly? Again, Mary stumbled in a turn but caught herself. It was a startling thought. However, it was also one which warranted consideration, for neither extreme was particularly laudable.

"I think we will sit out the second song," Darcy said as the song ended.

"I must apologize. I should be more attentive."

"There is no need to apologize. I am not as fond of dancing as some. I assure you that I am only disappointed for you if we sit out when you wished to dance."

She shook her head and laughed lightly. "I fear I am a danger to myself and everyone else when I am distracted. It does not happen often," she added quickly.

"Yes, I would place you as a very focused individual. We are much alike in that way also." He motioned to the side of the room, and Mary readily allowed him to escort her from the dance floor.

It was odd to think she was like anyone – especially someone as refined and dignified as Mr. Darcy. Her mother had always declared her as nearly the most unusual girl she had ever met. The prize for most unusual went to Elizabeth, of course. It seemed that in their mother's opinion, liking books and learning were far more strange than not wishing to trim every piece of clothing in ribbons and lace.

Mary truly did not mind a bit of embellishment, but flounces and excesses were, in her way of thinking, ridiculous. They would look out of place on her. She was far too serious for such frivolities. Any such statement disparaging finery was followed by a cry from her mother about how very odd she was. However, such oddness did have the benefit of keeping her mother from pushing Mary at any gentlemen at all. All of her other sisters would be put forward first, and then, there would be a moment of pause followed by a "well, there is Mary."

She was likely being too harsh on her mother. It was not as if her mother did not love her. She did.

Just as she loved Elizabeth. Had she not declared Mary to be very much like her father to Mrs. Salter that day in the store? It was just that her mother did not know how to relate to anyone who was not like Lydia, Kitty, or Jane.

Mary sighed. She would also need to consider if perhaps she held people to standards which were just not attainable and, much like her mother, was disparaging them for something which she could not understand.

She pulled on Mr. Darcy's arm as yet another thought sprang to mind.

He stopped and turned towards her. "Are you well?"

"I merely have a question and am afraid I might forget to ask you later if I wait."

"Very well. What do you wish to know?"

They were only a few feet from her sisters, so Mary lowered her voice. "You did not think well of my family when we first met."

His expression grew pained.

"How did you change your opinion? We have not changed. Or, at least, most of us have not changed. Lydia has."

"Love, and a good dose of misery," Darcy answered with a smile.

Her brow furrowed. Love she could understand, but misery?

"I attempted to give up your sister because of my disapproval of your family. They did not fit into my way of thinking, you see. I expected very particular behavior and looked down on those who did not meet my standards."

Mary's mouth popped open. Oh, she and Mr. Darcy were alike in many ways!

"It was Bingley who made me reconsider my miserable existence while I held firmly to my ideals and attempted to forget your sister."

"Mr. Bingley?"

Darcy nodded. "And once I admitted to myself that love was more important than those ideals, I began to see things differently. I began to understand better the motivations behind the behaviours which had before only been a source of annoyance." He shrugged. "I find I truly love your family now. I did not think it was possible at first, but I do." He made to lead her on to her sisters, but hesitated. "Was there anything else?"

She shook her head. "Not at present."

"I am available if and when you discover there is anything else."

"Thank you. You are not what I thought you were at first either."

"And what changed your opinion?" he asked as they approached Elizabeth.

"The way you love my sister," Mary whispered. "And my family, including me." Her cheeks burned at that admission.

"It is my pleasure." He turned from her. "Mr. Banks, have you met my wife and sisters?"

Finally, introductions were made, and Mary sighed in relief. Things were now as they should be.

"You did not complete your set. Are you well?" Elizabeth asked Mary when Mr. Banks had left them after securing a dance with Kitty.

"I was merely distracted."

"By what?" Elizabeth asked.

Mary shook her head, indicating that it was not at all important what she had been distracted by. "My thoughts."

Elizabeth's brow furrowed. "Do you wish to remain here?"

"Is Miss Mary ill?" Lady Matlock asked as she

and her husband along with Lydia joined them at that moment.

"No, I am just a bit pensive which has proved too much for my feet to handle while dancing."

Lady Matlock smiled. "Well, then, I think it might be best if we retired to Matlock House." She looked at Darcy. "You are welcome to join us."

"But what of..." his eyes flicked to Lydia and then Elizabeth, "my wife and sister's introduction to society."

Lady Matlock sighed. "You are right, of course, but if Mary is not feeling the thing, do you not think it best to leave before she stumbles?"

"I have already stumbled, my lady. Twice. It is why we are not dancing at present."

"But you did not fall, did you?"

Mary shook her head.

"We are at an impasse then."

"I would not mind if we left," Elizabeth inserted. "I have danced with my husband, what more is there to exceed such a treat tonight."

"A second dance with him," Mary offered.

Elizabeth shrugged. "There is that, but I would not be put out to miss it."

"And what of you, Miss Kitty?" Darcy asked.

"We will not leave until you have fulfilled your duty to Mr. Banks with the next set of dances. Do you wish to remain after that?"

Kitty surveyed the room before leaning forward and whispering, "I would like to be far away from that woman we met earlier."

"Which woman?" Elizabeth asked.

"Mrs. Salter," Mary replied. "She was rude."

Elizabeth laughed. "I would only be surprised if she were not."

"Then, we are in agreement?" A smirk that reminded Mary a good deal of Lord Westonbury's tipped Lady Matlock's lips. "Both about *that* woman and making a departure?"

"Yes," Kitty said before anyone else could reply.

"Well, then, Darcy, ask your wife to dance, and I will keep Miss Mary company until you are through, unless... My dear, do you think you could muster up enough reserves to dance with the handsomest gentleman in the room?" She batted her lashes at her husband. It was such a sweet gesture.

"But do you not wish to dance with him?" Mary asked.

Lady Matlock shook her head. "Not tonight."

Of its own accord, Mary's left eyebrow cocked in disbelief.

Lady Matlock laughed. "Very well, I would like to dance with him, but I will not leave you standing." Again, she smirked very much as her son did. "And I would very much like to carry the point Reginald began with *that* woman. There is no better way to announce your acceptance by the Earl of Matlock than to be seen dancing with him."

"Then, perhaps he should dance with Lydia."

"We have just taken a walk in the garden with Miss Lydia, and I made certain it was noticed."

Mary's brow furrowed. There were things she wished to sit and consider.

"I will not let you fall," Lord Matlock assured her. "Please?"

"Very well," Mary agreed. How did a lady turn down an earl when he truly seemed as if he wanted to dance with her?

Lady Matlock rubbed her hands together. "Excellent. Miss Lydia and I will sit right here and have a lovely discussion, will we not?'

"Oh, indeed!" Lydia cried eagerly – too eagerly. It was as if she was scheming.

Mary's eyes narrowed.

"We have that list to discuss," she gave Mary a pointed look. "There may be a name or two to add to it."

Mary was still not convinced that Lydia was being completely honest. She was using that sweet, innocent voice she used when she was hiding something. However, it could be the list she was hiding.

"I see Mr. Banks returning," Lord Matlock said. "Shall we cause a stir and take the floor first?"

"I would rather not," Mary replied and then pressed her lips together. She really did need to learn to keep her thoughts in her head long enough to weigh them before speaking.

Lord Matlock chuckled. "I am afraid Miss Mary that if you are to be a member of this family, you will have to harden yourself to the idea of being worthy of the notice of one and all on occasion. It is a danger of being tied to a titled gentleman." He took her hand. "I do not dance as much as I once did so my taking the floor with you will be noted." He bent his head in her direction and lowered his voice. "My wife is very good at carrying a point."

Mary chuckled at that.

"She is much like her son in that regard," Lord

Matlock added. "Neither would ever intentionally harm someone for whom they cared, and both would defend those they loved with a vehemence worthy of a mythical warrior." He smiled at her. "I know that is likely hard to believe considering Reginald's somewhat lackadaisical approach to life, but I assure you it is true. On our way home, I will tell you the story about how he broke his arm when he was nine. Someone made fun of Darcy." He winked at her and allowed her to take her place across from him.

Lord Matlock was wrong. She did not find it hard to believe that Lord Westonbury could be fiercely protective. She had heard him growl at Mrs. Salter and seen him tense as if he wished to do the lady bodily harm. Until that moment when she had witnessed Lord Westonbury's avenging side, she would not have believed what Lord Matlock had said. But now — Oh, dear! The first notes played as a very distracting thought captured Mary's mind. Perhaps she had judged him too harshly.

Chapter 14

"Good morning, my lord."

Wes turned his attention away from the window and, glancing toward Mary, gave a nod in greeting. He was only halfway through his cup of coffee and too caught up in his thoughts to speak. It was only early, but he had already been about some business and was contemplating his departure from Matlock House.

"Did you sleep well?"

Wes nodded in reply as Mary poured milk into her tea and moved her spoon backward and forward.

"My apologies," she said with a small grimace as her spoon clinked against the side of her cup.

Wes smiled and took a sip of his coffee. Careful. She was so careful. And particular. She was also very particular. Mary liked things to be done properly. He, on the other hand, had only truly cared for things to be done how he wished them to be or in such a fashion as to make his life least trying. It was a weak way to do things, he supposed, for it was much easier to glide through life, sliding around any impediment rather than taking the time and effort to either surmount the obstacle in one's way or abolish it. Of course, one could not always avoid unpleasantness in favour of the enjoyable, but until he had met her — the lady across from him who was carefully spreading cream so that not a bit of it exceeded the borders of her scone — until he had met her, he had done his best to find the most pleasant existence possible.

Mary lifted a spoon laden with jam, lifted a brow, and, after a quick glance at her scone, adjusted the amount of jam so that it was less.

Wes sighed and took another sip of his coffee. Moderation. Checks and balances. These were things at which Mary seemed to excel and which he needed to build up in himself. Pleasure was not wrong, unless that pleasure came at the expense of that which was truly worthy and valuable, and — he emptied the last of the coffee in his cup — the lady across from him was of extreme value. To be honored with her approval was a prize to be sought.

"Did you sleep well?" He settled back into his chair and prepared to watch her eat her breakfast. His had been devoured, but he was in no hurry to extricate himself from the pleasure of her presence. This was a pleasure that he counted amongst those of the best quality.

"I did. Thank you."

"You returned early from the ball." Indeed, he had been surprised to hear everyone in the halls before he had even settled into bed.

Was that a stain of pink on her cheeks? "You did not leave the soiree for some horrid reason, did you?"

"No, no," she assured him quickly. "The amusement of the evening waned after your departure."

"Was it because I had left?" he teased, expecting her to duck her head or roll her eyes. However, she did neither. She held his gaze and took a sip of tea from the very fortunate cup she held before her lips.

"Yes."

He blinked. Had she said yes?

"You are very vexing," she scolded.

"So I have been told." His brow furrowed. "Might I inquire as to what in particular was vexing?"

She smiled. "There are so many options, my lord."

A tease? She had favoured him with a tease? How tantalizingly lovely.

"As it relates to yesterday's ball," he clarified. "The rest can wait until a later date or be forgotten altogether. In fact, it is likely best if they are forgotten."

She nodded. "It is likely best, but I am not certain it is entirely possible."

He shrugged. "It is worth an attempt."

"Trust me, my lord. I have been attempting to remove the more vexing thoughts about you from my memory. It is not easily done." Her lips lost their amused curl and her eyes grew serious. "However, I may have been somewhat mistaken in my opinions."

Wes's eyebrows jumped upward. "How so?"

"Well, for one, I had not considered that you would care for anyone save yourself. I truly did not think it possible after hearing about how you first greeted my sisters and then how casually you presented yourself upon our first meeting."

He would have been greatly offended by such comments had he not been watching her turn the handle of her cup away and back, her eyes following the motion. A blush stained her cheeks. She was not speaking harshly. She was being truthful. Painfully truthful. And he could not fault her first assessment of his character. It had been wanting.

"However," she continued, sparing him a quick glance before once again watching her hands fiddle with her cup and then, her saucer, "since then, I have seen your care for your brother, and, though your interactions with your mother do want some improvement, I can see that you only push as far as being excessively annoying and, I would venture, rarely to the point of doing harm. And you do seem to do as she asks, though not always without some rejoinder or other irritation."

"That is just how we are." He and his mother had always had such a relationship. She would instruct, and he would try her patience before doing what she had asked or something very close to what she had asked.

"I know that now that I have seen beyond the

public rooms." Her eyes lifted to his. "I am not here to scold you about such things. However, I will ask you not to interrupt until I have concluded. This is not easily done."

"I will do my best but cannot promise to succeed."

She shook her head. "I must admit that you are very honest with me."

"I have promised to be so."

She gave him a pointed look.

"My apologies," he said before pressing his lips together.

"That is another thing which surprises me. You do not make a promise lightly."

"Never," he said before once again making a show of firmly pressing his lips together.

"You are not who I thought you were. I am somewhat pleasantly surprised."

This was a good thing!

"And yet it is entirely vexing. How you defended myself and my sisters to Mrs. Salter, coupled with your admission about your friend, Mr. Langley, had me at sixes and sevens. Both took me by surprise." She looked up at him again. "I nearly fell while dancing with Darcy because of you."

She had been thinking about him while dancing with his cousin, had she? He was hopeful that such a thing was a good thing.

"Thankfully, I did not stumble as much when I danced with Lord Matlock."

"You danced with my father?" His father rarely danced these days and usually only with his mother.

The door to the morning room opened, drawing his attention, but then closed without anyone entering or exiting.

"One does not refuse an earl," Mary replied.

"Just a viscount," Wes muttered.

"Only if he asks for a second dance," Mary retorted.

There was a familiar edge of scolding to her tone which he found surprisingly welcome.

"It was while I was dancing with your father when I came to the conclusion that I might have judged you too harshly – not unfairly, but too harshly."

"Are they not the same thing?"

She shook her head and took up her cup of tea. "Not at all. My assessment of your actions as inap-propriate where they pertain to my sisters and visiting a brothel are not unjust. Neither is commendable. However, it might be not within your power to –"

"You think I am incapable of being anything other than I have been?" Wes interrupted. Had they not progressed at all in their friendship?

"Not precisely. I had not considered your nature. For some, such as myself, it is far easier to abide by rules, for others, it is a challenge."

"You think that I would struggle to be honorable if I should by some miracle of heaven choose to be?" He knew he should likely not use such a harsh tone with her, but his aching heart would not allow his good sense to overrule it.

Her expression became pained. "No, no, that is not it precisely. At least I do not think it is. I just know that being unfair and harsh are not the same."

"Thank you for clarifying your opinion of me," Wes snapped.

"I did not mean to hurt you." She blinked as if fighting tears. "The point to which I wished to come," her voice was unsteady and filled with emotion, "is that with this new understanding of things, I should welcome your friendship."

"You would welcome the friendship of a gentleman who has very little hope of ever being honorable?"

Her eyes, which were watery, flashed. Whatever compassion she might have felt for him seemed to flee at his comment.

"I am certain you are perfectly capable of being whatever you wish to be." She stood. "With any luck, you will be as successful at whatever you chose as you are at being vexing." She turned away from him

He should stop her from leaving the room, but as it happened, she was apparently not finished with venting her displeasure and turned back to him.

"You seemed eager last evening, after telling me of your duplicity regarding your friend, to know if we remained friends." She brushed a tear from her cheek, and his heart clenched. "I was uncertain at that time if we should, but then came to the conclusion which I have just related to you." She brushed at tears again and shook her head before spinning from him and dashing out of the room.

Wes leapt to his feet. "Mary," he called after her, but she did not stop.

"What have you done?" his mother questioned, catching him by the arm as he left the room.

"I will go to her," Lydia, who was standing next to his mother just outside the breakfast room door, offered.

"No, I will go," Wes said.

"You cannot," Lydia protested.

"I must. It is but disagreement." He pulled his arm free from his mother and raced up the stairs after Mary. He caught up to her just as she was about to reach her room. "Mary, please," he begged. "Do not let us part like this."

She stopped but did not turn toward him.

"Forgive me." That seemed the best place to start. "Please."

Her shoulders lifted and lowered, but she did not run from him. So, he ventured to take a step nearer her.

"You are correct."

She dared to peek at him. The tracks of tears on her cheeks tore at him, and he swiftly wrapped her in his embrace.

"My lord!"

"I know it is improper," he assured her. "But I

have hurt you most grievously and cannot help but attempt to provide comfort."

She struggled against his embrace for only a moment before she seemed to lose all strength and leaned into him willingly. If the circumstances which preceded such a thing were not what they were, Wes would have very much enjoyed her reliance on his strength to support her.

"You were correct that I will struggle with behaving as I wish."

"I should not have said it."

"No, no, you were right to tell me. I would have you be honest with me even if it does pain me to hear of my shortcomings."

"I am sorry," she whispered.

"Will you still be my friend?" His breath caught in his chest for the moment it took for her to reply with a nod of her head.

"Do you think it is possible we can be?" she asked.

As much as he did not wish to, he released her from his embrace, but he kept hold of one of her hands and did not move away from her. "Why would it not be possible?"

"I am so very disagreeable."

With his free hand, he pulled out his handkerchief and dried her cheek. "I have not used it. It will not contaminate you."

She gave a little laugh.

"You are given to lecturing. I will not deny that." He attempted to soften his words with a smile, which was returned. "However, friends can argue. They can even get angry to the point of wishing to call the other out as Langley did." Her eyes widened, and he nodded. "It seems I have a propensity to anger those I care about at times."

"In that we are equals," she admitted.

"Has someone called you out?"

She giggled. "No, but I assure you, I have made my sisters angry with me many times." Her lips tipped into a sheepish grin. "And I have already confessed to purposefully trying my mother's nerves."

"To keep from being put forward." He remembered their first civil conversation in the library on the day he discovered she was staying here.

"We are alike in that way as well," she said. "We both vex our mothers, though for different reasons."

"Then, it stands to reason that two such vexing

people would, on occasion, come to blows – not literal blows but I think you understand my meaning?" He placed a finger under her chin and lifted it so he could see her eyes. "I not only promise to be always honest with you but also to always do my best to right any wrong. Do you forgive me?"

She pulled her lower lip between her teeth while a smile pulled at those lips and fresh tears formed in her eyes. "I will, and will you forgive me?"

He nodded as he was not certain he was capable of speech at the moment due to the light of happiness in her eyes at having their friendship restored.

"And you will not turn me away for being too difficult?"

Wes blinked. "Why should I do that?"

Mary shrugged. "Most do."

He lifted her hand to his lips. "I am not like most."

"My lord!" she scolded as she snatched her hand from him after he kissed it. "That is not proper."

"It will be a struggle." He favoured her with a teasing grin.

She shook her head. "You do not seem to be trying very hard."

"I assure you I am succeeding far more than you

know." Every fiber in his being wished to kiss her at that moment, especially when she cocked that skeptical brow. "And I did promise to always be honest with you, so you must believe me."

"That will be a struggle."

He had no doubt it would be. Mary seemed the sort to question a report that it was raining even if the report was given by a man carrying an umbrella and dripping water on her floor.

"You did not finish your breakfast. Shall I bring it up to you?"

"In my room?"

Could eyes grow wider and more shocked than hers were right now?

"No, no, that would be very improper," he assured her. "Then, would you like to join me in returning to the breakfast room so that my mother can see that I have not caused any lasting damage?"

Her shoulders lifted and lowered as she drew and released a breath. "I would like that very much, for I am hungry. However, I would like to wash my face first."

"Take whatever time you need. I shall wait for you at the top of the stairs." He stood where he was and watched her traverse the few remaining steps to her room. Then, he took himself to the grand staircase and sat down on the top step to wait for her.

Chapter 15

"It is a delight to have such a notable person call on us, Lord Westonbury." Mrs. Gardiner tucked a basket of stitching under her chair. "We have not seen you since the wedding"

"He insisted on joining us," Mary grumbled.

"We are family," Wes countered. He also wished to demonstrate to Miss Glower-at-the-Viscount – there was something rather charming about her glower — that he was not above her relatives in trade. His aunt Catherine might not agree with such a sentiment, but he rarely cared what his aunt Catherine thought was or was not proper. She was perhaps the most taxing of all his relations to tolerate. However, she was also the easiest to rile, and there was some entertainment in that.

"My mother was sorry that she was unable to join us," he added when taking a seat. "However, I am to extend an invitation for you to call on her at Matlock House whenever your schedule allows for such."

"There were some items regarding the menu and room décor which demanded Lady Matlock's attention today," Lydia explained. She leaned toward her aunt. "It is very much the same as what Mama would be doing only in a far larger house with a greater number of staff."

"That is good to know," Mrs. Gardiner replied. "I have often wondered how those in the upper circles do things." She turned to Wes. "I am fascinated by such things. For instance, how is tea served in the palace or on an East Indiaman? One hears reports, of course, but reports may or may not be accurate."

"That is very true, although I cannot say I ever really considered such things," Wes admitted.

"We are all different. What one finds interesting another considers a complete drudgery," Mrs. Gardiner assured him. "And I will dare to offend by saying it is likely a woman who contemplates the intricacies of how things in a home are done more than the man. I know that is not patently true in all cases but in general, I think it is."

"I am not offended, nor do I disagree," Wes replied.

"You do not?"

"No, Miss Mary, I do not."

Her left eyebrow arched, and her lips pursed. He knew she wanted more of an explanation. He, on the other hand, wanted to admire her puckered lips rather than speak further. However, that would be vexing, and vexing Mary too much often led to her avoiding him for a time, which was not the desired outcome.

"I am fully aware that it is the lady of the house upon whom the weight of entertaining and seeing to home comforts falls." Ah, a smile. Not a large one, but a smile, nonetheless. He had impressed her.

"You do have some surprisingly astute observations, my lord."

He chuckled. Her teases were even more delightful than her scowls. "I try to keep my astuteness hidden. Not everyone admires a quick mind."

She shook her head, but she continued to smile. There was an easiness which seemed to be settling in around them since they had come to an agreement about friendship two days ago after their quarrel at breakfast.

"How is the colonel?" Mrs. Gardiner's eyes were dancing with amusement as she looked first at Mary and then Wes.

"He is to join us later for a drive in the park," Wes answered.

"His head hurts less each day," Lydia added. "But I thought it might be too much for him to both visit and drive."

Wes truly had never thought he would see the day when his little brother would be so easily swayed by a suggestion. The fact that the suggestion came from such a lovely young lady as Lydia Bennet made it understandable even if it was surprising. He glanced at Mary and imagined he would not be quite as obliging. His lips tipped upwards as a new thought contradicted his first. He might be very obliging if he were to be favoured with her kisses as he knew his brother was favoured with Lydia's. They were circumspect, but they had not been so cautious that he had not witnessed a kiss or two.

"And his eyesight?" Mrs. Gardiner asked. "Has it improved?"

Lydia shook her head.

Mrs. Gardiner clucked her tongue. "That must be very trying."

Wes had to agree with that. He could not imagine not being able to see if there was someone at his side without turning his head to do so.

"He says it is not so strange as it once was," Lydia said.

"Our bodies are quite wonderful things. They can adapt when needed," Mrs. Gardiner said.

A maid stepped into the room. "The table is laid, ma'am."

"Very good. We will be in straightaway." She turned back to her guests. "We are taking tea with my children, and I never do that in here." She rose. "They are just learning their manner, my lord," she cautioned.

"I will do my best to remember mine," he assured her as he followed her out of the room and down the hall to a modest-sized dining room.

The table could easily seat ten people, twelve if needed, and if the table were to be longer, a party of sixteen would not be too tight in a room of this size. Sideboards stood on either side of the table and a fireplace stood at the head. It was a cheerful, homely room with a distinct touch of elegance.

"See to your sister, Albert," Mrs. Gardiner instructed.

Albert was the only one of the four children, who stood not-so-patiently waiting for their mother, who had earned the privilege of wearing breeches. Without a second word from his mother, the youngster, who was nearly a full head shorter than his sister, offered her his arm and escorted her to a chair, which he pulled out for her.

"Hugh. John. You may take your places."

The remaining two youngsters scurried to climb up on chairs. No doubt, they were eager to be given their tea and cake.

"And now for us adults," Mrs. Gardiner said. "It is not how precedence works in normal circumstances, but when one does not wish to upset trays and pots, it is best to seat the children first."

Wes could imagine the capers that three young chaps could get up to without someone to keep them focused on the task at hand.

"Children," Mrs. Gardiner continued as the others took their seats. "I do not wish for you to bow or curtsey since we are already seated for tea, but

I would like you to meet Lord Westonbury. He is Mr. Darcy's cousin."

"Like Mary?" the nearly youngest boy asked.

"And Idia?" the youngest boy asked.

Which was Hugh and which was John was not yet clear to Wes.

"Yes, like Lydia and Mary are your cousins, Lord Westonbury is Mr. Darcy's cousin." She smiled at Wes. "I do hope you are not offended by the informality of your introduction."

"Not at all," he assured her. "I am delighted to meet your children."

"Thank you, my lord. The eldest, and my only daughter thus far, is Carissa. She turned seven just three months ago. Next, is Albert, who will be six next month. Then, there is Hugh who is nearly four, and John, who is two." She nodded to her children who did their best to each say, "It is a pleasure to meet you, Lord Westonbury."

The eldest two did very well with the task. However, the two youngest struggled, and John had to be helped along three times before he could get all the words out in the order they needed to be and pronounced in a way that was distinguishable, although Wes did remain Ord Estonbawy, which his mother allowed to be shortened to *my ord*. Apparently, *L* was a letter the child had not yet mastered.

"We have some exciting news to share with you, Mary and Lydia," Mrs. Gardiner said as she poured tea — half cups for the children, which were left in the middle of the table to cool, and then full cups for the adults, who were allowed to accept them while still hot.

"Would you like to share our news with your cousins, Carissa?"

The young girl's head bobbed up and down. "Mama is going to have a baby."

"She is?" Lydia cried with delight.

"That is wonderful," Mary said with obvious pleasure.

"He will be an early Christmas present," Albert said.

"*She* will be an early Christmas present," Carissa corrected.

"As you can imagine, my lord, my daughter is eager to have a sister."

"I can understand that." Wes could imagine how trying it must be to have three younger brothers.

"Do you have any sisters, my lord?" Carissa asked.

"No, I only have one brother."

"Only one?" Albert appeared aghast at the thought.

"Yes, only one."

"That could not be very much fun," Albert said.

"Ah, but we often had Mr. Darcy with whom to play."

"He has a sister," Carissa inserted.

"He does indeed. She is a very sweet young lady."

"Like Rissa," Hugh said around a bit of cake.

"I imagine that is true, though I do not know your sister so well as to be an excellent judge, she does strike me as being sweet."

Carissa beamed while Hugh's head bobbed up and down as he assured Wes that she was.

"Most of the time," Albert muttered, earning him a glare from his mother.

Wes leaned forward and lowered his voice. "I will have a sister when my brother gets married."

Albert wrinkled his nose at the idea, but Carissa and the others seemed delighted with the notion.

"And," Wes continued, "she is a very nice young lady."

"What is she like?" Carissa asked.

Wes looked at Lydia. "A great deal like your cousin Miss Lydia."

Four pairs of curious eyes turned toward Lydia.

"My lord," Mary whispered in her lovely scolding tone, which, after enjoying hearing it, he ignored.

"This cannot be spoken of outside of our family, for nothing has been officially announced."

The curious eyes turned back toward him and each nodded their agreement, though John looked somewhat confused as to what was actually happening.

"My future sister is not just a lot like your cousin, she will be your cousin, for my brother plans to marry Miss Lydia." He held up a hand. "Although I am unaware of any official offer."

"Is it true?" Carissa asked Lydia, who nodded.

"When the colonel has healed more then we can discuss marrying."

"He is a colonel?" Albert was suddenly impressed with the situation.

"He is, but he was injured."

"Where?" Albert asked eagerly.

"That is not polite," Mrs. Gardiner scolded.

"He had several wounds, which we must not speak about during tea. They can be off-putting, and no one wishes to have their cakes ruined," Wes said. "However, it is his head which still troubles him for he sustained a great blow to it." He looked very seriously at young Albert. "I am fortunate to still have a brother."

Albert's eyes grew wide, and Wes saw him swallow as he looked at his younger brothers. That's exactly how Wes had felt when he had heard that Richard had been injured. He could not imagine his life without his younger brother, and, until that moment when he had read the letter informing his parents of Richard's injury, the full gravity of his brother's profession had not engulfed him with worry. That was why he had been the first to arrive at Netherfield. He could not wait to receive news from Darcy as his mother suggested. He needed to know about his brother's welfare as soon as he possibly could.

"A soldier's work is dangerous," Wes added.

Albert nodded.

"Are you a soldier?" Carissa asked.

"No."

"Then, what are you?"

Wes sat back in his chair. That was a good question. "I am a lord."

"What does a lord do?' Albert asked.

That was also a good question and one for which he did not have a good answer. "I am not rightly sure," he answered honestly. What did he do other than pleasing himself with entertainment?

"I imagine," Mary answered. "that a lord learns. First, he must learn all there is to know at school. Then, he must learn all he can about life and the government, for one day, he will have to take his seat in the House of Lords where it will be his duty to see that England prospers, and it will also be his duty to take part in decisions which will deploy the army as needed. Being a lord is no easy task."

Wes was certain his eyes were as wide as Alberts to hear what a lord should do.

"I am not certain that is what all lords do," he said.

"I would agree. However, I am certain that is what the best ones do." She batted her lashes at him.

Was she challenging him to take his title seriously and give up his life of frivolity? And with an audience of impressionable children as witnesses and, in front of whom, he could not argue with her? He smiled. Oh, his mother would be impressed.

"Miss Mary is exactly right, but then again," he turned his eyes from Mary and back to his eager audience, "she is a rather clever lady, is she not?"

Chapter 16

"I should like to visit your cousins again."

Mary turned her eyes from watching the people in the park to the gentleman sitting next to her and across from his brother. That was the third time he had mentioned her cousins since leaving the Gardiner house. He had appeared rather enamored of them when they were at her aunt's house. He had even seemed reluctant to let them depart to the nursery when tea was over. Apparently, it was not a passing fancy but a true approbation for children.

"Have you had tea with children?" he asked his brother.

"No, I cannot say that I have beyond having tea with Georgiana when she was younger."

Lord Westonbury shook his head. "That does not count."

"Why?"

"She was not young enough."

"I guarantee you she was young," Richard protested.

"But so were you."

Richard shrugged. "I suppose."

"To clarify," Mary interrupted in a rather sardonic tone, "my lord, wishes to know if you have had tea with children less than the age of twelve since reaching your majority plus, what five years?" She looked at Lord Westonbury who was to her utter annoyance smiling. She was still a trifle put out with him for joining them at the Gardiners, and it was hard to remain so when he had been so charming with her cousins, as well as obliging all day.

"Yes, yes, I believe five years would be just the correct number." He turned back to his brother.

She wished to tell him to stop agreeing with her so she could remain irritated with him, but that would be rather small of her, now, would it not?

"No, I have not," Richard replied.

"Then, you must come with us next time. Master Gardiner would be delighted to meet a soldier –"

"I am no longer a soldier."

Lord Westonbury waved the comment away.

"But you were, and Master Gardiner was quite interested in soldiers." He opened his mouth and then closed it as Mary watched his expression grow serious. "It would be good for him to see what can happen to a soldier. It is a noble profession, do not mistake me, but..." He shook his head. "I am not sorry you have been required to give it up." The left side of his mouth tipped up, and he shrugged. "I rather like having you for a brother."

Mary could not help but smile at the way Lord Westonbury seemed to care so much for his brother. Whatever his lord held dear was held with fierceness and abandon. One did not have to wonder where his loyalties lay. If it were not for his fondness of brothels, she could very easily be persuaded to like him. It was a good thing then that he had that mark against him, for, with it, she was in little danger of losing her heart. Or so she hoped.

"When my head allows it, I will join you one day," Richard assured him. "I will admit that with the continued unrest in the north, as well as on the continent, my loss of vision may indeed be a blessing in disguise." He blew out a breath. "I find that with each passing day, I regret the loss of my profession less and less."

He lifted Lydia's fingers to his lips, and Mary turned away. Not because it was improper or something of which she disapproved. No. It was because she found herself longing to be so loved. It was easier to deal with the ache in her heart when she was not witnessing such sweet gestures as the kissing of fingers. She was happy for Lydia. Truly, she was, but her happiness was mingled with a touch of jealousy.

"Are you well?" Lord Westonbury had leaned toward her so he could whisper in her ear.

"Yes, I am well," she assured him.

"You looked sad."

"Pensive," she corrected.

"And of what were you thinking?"

She shook her head. "Nothing of significance," she lied.

He tipped his head and studied her face. "Are you certain?" His voice said he did not believe her.

She closed her eyes and shook her head. He had promised to be honest with her, and she would honor that promise by returning his honesty. She opened her eyes and looked into his. "No," she admitted. "However, I prefer not to discuss it."

"I will not tease you or think you strange."

"You cannot promise that," she retorted. Teasing was in his very nature. There was no removing it from him. Such a separation of lightness from the more serious side of his personality was just not possible.

"Then, you think I will tease you for whatever it is which to think about makes you look sad."

There was a hint of hurt in his tone.

"No... well, perhaps, but not because I think you are cruel or some such thing."

"Well, that is good, I suppose." He did not sound convinced.

"This is just not the appropriate time or place to discuss such things."

"Then, will you tell me later?"

"No."

"Why?"

"Because I do not wish to tell you. It is a private matter which is best kept to myself." She held his gaze. His lips puckered slightly, and a small furrow appeared between his eyes. He was not pleased with her reply, but that was unfortunate because there was no way she was going to tell him that she was jealous of her sister's good fortune in being loved. That was something she was not going to tell anyone.

"Very well," he finally agreed after a full minute of staring her down.

Goodness, he was obstinate!

"You have pretty eyes," he added with a smirk.

Was that what he was doing? Admiring her eyes? Was he not attempting to wait until she gave in and told him her secret? Oh, he was frustrating. She smiled. And sweet. No one had ever told her she had pretty eyes before. Of course, that was likely because no one had taken the time to stare into them as he had just done.

"Thank you."

"There is great deal about you which is pleasing."

Mary's cheeks grew warm.

"Would you care for me to elaborate?"

"No."

"Why?"

Oh, he was incorrigible!

"I am certain my sister and your brother did not agree to come on this drive so that you could spend the whole time flattering me for who knows what purpose."

"I do not mind," Lydia interrupted. "I would find it delightful to hear what Lord Westonbury finds pleasing about you."

"No, you would not." Mary gave her sister a pointed look. Lydia was wearing that secret smile of hers which never led to anything good. She might be maturing, but her desire to poke her nose in where it did not belong seemed to be unchanged.

"My dear," Colonel Fitzwilliam reproved softly.

Lydia sighed. "If that is what you wish."

"It is," Mary assured her.

"But..."

Mary groaned.

"I have never heard a gentleman enumerate what he likes about you. I have heard such things about Jane and Kitty..." Her head tipped to the side as her face puckered in thought. "And quite recently, Lizzy." She sighed. "Mr. Darcy quite loves her, you know."

"I should hope he does since he married her," Mary quipped.

Lydia raised a disapproving brow at Mary. "But I have yet to hear such things about you."

"Truly?"

Lord Westonbury sounded shocked by such a revelation, though it should not be so difficult to believe. She was plain and lacked the liveliness of Lydia and Lizzy, as well as the sweetness of Jane and Kitty, and her accomplishments were not great. Her sense of fashion was acceptable but not worthy of note, and her hair was... well... just hair. Something which covered her head, but neither spun gold nor the colour of honey nor did it blaze with the colours of a flaming sunset. Her noteworthy traits were sardonic humor and an occasionally acerbic tongue. Neither of those things was deserving of praise.

"Well, then, you have been surrounded by fools – Darcy, Bingley, and my brother not included, of course – but the rest of those eligible gentlemen who have not noticed your excellent qualities are most decidedly fools." His lips tipped up. "Though I cannot be too harsh on them, for if they had possessed the good sense to recognize what a treasure you are, then I would not be riding in the carriage with you on such a fine day, and that would be a great travesty."

Mary rolled her eyes. "My lord, have you forgotten your pledge of truthfulness?"

"Not at all, and if you would allow me to do so, I would tell you all the things which such fools have missed."

"Wes," once again the colonel intervened with a soft reprimand, not that it was as effective on his brother as it had been on Lydia.

"Please?" Lord Westonbury pleaded.

Once again, Mary found herself holding his gaze. "One thing," she said. "You may tell me one thing beyond my eyes which you find pleasant about me, and then, we will enjoy our ride without any further unsettling conversations." Goodness! She sounded as if she was a governess instructing her charge. How he could find anything to admire about her when she was so frequently disagreeable was beyond her.

"It is unsettling to hear praise?" Lord Westonbury asked.

"Yes."

"That is odd," he muttered.

"Maybe for you, but not for me."

"How so?"

"Look at you." She waved a hand up and then down, indicating his person.

"I cannot see me. I have no mirror."

She scowled at him, which only made him smile more.

"You are far too comfortable with praise, my lord."

"I do not think that is possible."

"You do not have to agree for it to be true."

"Then, explain it to me."

"The last time I attempted to explain something to you, it did not end well," she cautioned.

"I am willing to try to understand without offense."

"Very well. You are a lord."

"Yes, I am. We discussed that over tea." He held up a finger. "And I intend to be a good one, now that I know what one does."

"You did not know what a lord does?" Richard asked in disbelief.

"I had not heard it explained as succinctly as Miss Mary explained it today."

"I am sure it is nothing more than what your father likely attempted to teach you," Mary said. "My apologies. That was not kind." She really needed to keep her thoughts in her head better. But he seemed to provoke her in such a way that it was nearly impossible to do so.

"No, you are correct. If he had been as pretty as you, I am certain I would have paid better attention."

"My lord!"

"You are pretty. Even Langley thinks so. It is not just me."

"Mr. Langley thinks I am pretty?"

"Yes." He scowled.

"Indeed?"

"You are pleased that Langley thought you pretty, but you refuse to hear such from me?"

Oh, they were headed down a dangerous path. "I am just surprised."

"Did he not tell you he thought you were pretty when he called on you?"

"No. He complimented my ensemble and said I looked well."

"That is what a gentleman does if he is calling on you and thinks you are pretty," Lydia inserted.

"Exactly!" Lord Westonbury agreed.

"It is what one does if one is being polite," Mary protested.

"But it means more when a gentleman is calling on you," Lydia said.

"Truly?" There was so much she did not know about the whole process of being courted.

"How do you not know that?"

"I have never had a suitor, my lord." Her cheeks burned, and tears pricked her eyes.

"Fools!" Lord Westonbury cried. "The world is full of daft fools."

Mary shook her head. He was not teasing, yet it felt as if he was.

"I believe it with all my heart," he said softly while taking her hand. "I cannot imagine how they have overlooked you. I could not."

She blinked. Was he saying he wished to court her? That could not be. It simply would not work. She had requirements for gentlemen, and he... well... he did not meet them. It pained her heart to think it. "Which, I suppose, is why we are *friends*?"

He released her hand, and his features fell. "Yes."

It was a small word which was nearly whispered, but, though she was not experienced in the art of courting, even she knew it was all the proof she needed to know he had hoped for a different reply. She brushed at a wayward tear.

"To return to my explanation." She took a breath. "You have a title and a fortune. You are amiable and truly entertaining. And I think it goes without saying that you are handsome. Such things have made praise a normal, comfortable, and even expected part of your life."

He nodded and turned away. "And yet it is not enough," he murmured.

"For what?" Mary whispered, fearful of his answer.

He turned toward her. "For you." Then, he turned away from her again while her heart shattered at the pain she had seen in his eyes.

Chapter 17

Mary stepped out of the library and looked up and down the corridor. There was no one there save for a footman going about his duties. It must have been his steps she had heard. She should just go to her room and pretend to read. It was not as if sitting in the library with the door open and flipping the pages of a book had gained her the result for which she wished. Lord Westonbury had disappeared as soon as they had arrived home from their drive in the park, and she had not seen him since.

"Perhaps he will be at dinner," Lydia said, coming to stand behind Mary in the hall.

"What do you mean?" Mary asked in surprise.

"You have been watching the door for an hour. I think we both know for whom you are watching." Lydia put an arm around Mary's shoulder. "Do you wish to go to your room before we go to the drawing room? Lizzy and Kitty will be arriving soon if they are not already here."

"Is it so late already?" It had seemed like forever since they had returned from their drive, and yet, it had seemed like it was only a moment. Being engaged in scolding one's self seemed to make one's mind forget much else other than the thing which must be done to make amends. Not that Mary had figured out exactly how to best do that, for how did one make amends for being afraid?

"It is." Lydia squeezed Mary close. "Are you well? You never lose track of time."

Mary sighed deeply. "No." She had no desire to attempt to deny that she was feeling a great deal less than well. Her nerves seemed to be always on edge, and her heart did not seem to know which way was right and which was wrong. "I want to go home."

"You want to do what?"

"I want to go home. I cannot do this." Mary shrugged out of Lydia's embrace and began walking quickly down the hall toward the staircase.

"You cannot do what?" Lydia sounded exasperated as she hurried after her.

"Kitty can come to stay with you. You do not need me. I am sure Mama is likely growing bored with an empty house."

"She has Jane to visit."

"Yes, but how fair it that to Jane? One of us should be there to divert Mama from time to time, and since town does not seem to agree with me as well as it does with you and Kitty, I think it is I who should go home."

Lydia caught her by the arm just as they reached the stairs. "You cannot do what?"

"This." Mary held Lydia's gaze, refusing to explain any further.

"I do not know what *this* is." Lydia's eyes narrowed as Mary remained silent.

Below them, Mary could hear the door opening and the Darcys arriving.

"We need to go down," she said to Lydia.

"Not until you tell me what *this* is."

"We should not make our sisters and Mr. Darcy wait for us."

"Then, I suggest you answer my question with something more than the word this."

"Is the colonel meeting you downstairs, or are you waiting for him here?"

"That will not work," Lydia's scowl deepened.

"What will not work?" Mary attempted to sound as confused as possible.

"You are not going to divert me from the fact that you have not answered my question."

Mary huffed. "You are excessively obstinate!"

"Nearly as obstinate as you!" Lydia retorted.

"Ladies." Lady Matlock was standing at the bottom of the staircase. "Is there a problem?"

"No," Mary replied while at the same time Lydia said, "yes."

"Well, it cannot be both." Lady Matlock started up the stairs toward them.

"We need to go," Mary hissed to Lydia.

"Not until you tell me," Lydia whispered back.

"Are you arguing about anything in particular?" Lady Matlock was about halfway up the stairs.

Again, Mary replied no while Lydia said yes.

"I have been a mother for more years than either of you have been alive, and although I did not have daughters, I am perfectly capable of seeing that you are not pleased with each other." She had reached them by this time and, taking Mary by the arm, began steering her back toward the library and away from the staircase. "I will not have my dinner party ruined by a fit of ill-temper."

"She wants to go home," Lydia blurted.

"I beg your pardon?" Lady Matlock asked in surprise.

"Mary wants to go home."

"Why is that?" Lady Matlock asked Mary.

"I am not suited for town, my lady. It was a bad idea for me to come."

"Being ill-at-ease in town does not make one ill-suited for it. It means one must acquire the skills necessary for the task."

Mary shook her head. "I cannot..."

Lady Matlock looked at Mary as if she was waiting for her to continue.

But what was it precisely that she could not do? Mary had no answer to give, or, at least, she did not have one which she wished to give.

"I just cannot," Mary replied.

"Can you dance?"

"Yes, my lady."

"Can you entertain callers in a drawing room?"

"Yes, my lady."

"Do you think you will be able to sit through a play and enjoy it?"

"I am nearly certain I can."

"Can you endure being seen in the park during the busy hour?"

"I would rather not."

"But you can do it, can you not?"

"Yes, my lady."

"Can you ignore the gossips such as Mrs. Salter? Or do you care too much for what they say?"

"I do not care one whit what Mrs. Salter says," Mary said sharply. If there was one thing she could not abide it was women such as Mrs. Salter who stirred up trouble by telling tales, but it was not as if she felt such tales were worthy of cowering from. Shrinking from such tongue-wagging only gave power and credence to the gossip and gossiper.

"Then, what is it that you cannot do?"

Mary shrugged. She had a good notion of what it was, but she was not certain she wished to say.

"Can you love?" Lady Matlock's voice was soft and soothing.

"Yes, my lady."

"Fiercely?"

Mary nodded. That was why she had been so angry with Lord Westonbury. She loved her sisters with great fervour, and he had not treated them well.

"Can you love my son?"

The top of Mary's head grew cold, followed by her face, and neck as the blood drained from them and raced down towards her heart which seemed to be thudding rather loudly. Mary struggled to draw a deep breath. Fear coursed through her veins. Could she love Lord Westonbury?

"Sit," Lady Matlock commanded.

Mary looked at the chair behind her. How had she gotten to it? She did not recollect moving, but she gratefully sank onto the chair.

"He is not what you expected."

It was not a question, yet, Mary nodded. He was not at all the sort of gentleman whom she had ever wished to love.

"But you love him," Lady Matlock continued.

Tears gathered in Mary's eyes, and she shook her head in opposition to what her heart cried. "I cannot." Her voice was weak and raspy.

Lady Matlock took Mary's face in her hands and held it so that she could look directly into Mary's eyes just as Mary had seen her aunt do with her children when they were beside themselves because of something. It was a very comforting and reassuring feeling.

"Miss Bennet, you will find that if your heart is engaged, as I suspect it is, that you will not be able to not love him."

No. It could not be that she loved Lord Weston-bury. They were friends. That was all. Tears spilled down her cheeks. She could not love him, for if she did... She shook her head. "I am afraid," she whispered.

Lady Matlock, who still held her face in her hands, bent forward and kissed her forehead. "We all are at one point," she whispered. "Often, the things which scare us the most are the ones which will bring us the greatest joy. Talk to him. Tell him of your fear."

Mary shook her head.

"You must." Lady Matlock stood. "Just as you must wash your face and join us for dinner." She smoothed her skirts. "I will escort your sister down to the drawing room. Do not be long. I, for one, am hungry."

Mary returned Lady Matlock's smile and then went to do as instructed.

~*~*~

Lord Westonbury was not at dinner.

The fact should have put Mary's mind at ease since she would not have to look at him while unsettling thoughts from what his mother had said scurried around her mind, bumping into this memory and that, but it did not.

It was a very quiet dinner for Mary. She said barely a word and attended to only a few more than she spoke. No one seemed to do much more than cast a questioning look her way. Not one person pressed her to join a conversation. They gave her time and space to ponder.

By the time dessert was placed before her, Mary was utterly certain that she loved Lord Westonbury and not as a friend loves a friend. She had replayed his defense of his brother, as well as of her and Lydia, to Mrs. Salter. In the exchange, the ferocity of his love had shone as brightly as a torch at midnight. She could remember how his father had said something very much like that when she had danced with Lord Matlock.

She swept the last bite of cake off her fork while her eyes watched Mr. Darcy tip his head and study Elizabeth while wearing a besotted smile, and his words about the misery which attempting to not love Elizabeth had brought him came to mind.

She sighed and shook her head as she returned her fork to the table. Mr. Darcy's accepting a family of foolish people, though not a simple task, was nothing compared to meshing her belief that a gentleman should treat women with respect and love only his wife with Lord Westonbury's actions toward her sisters and his having a mistress.

Had. She heard him say to Mrs. Salter. *I had a mistress.* He had then declared that the arrangement was no longer in place. How had she not considered those words before and asked him about it? Had he truly dismissed his mistress? And for how long?

She groaned as she remembered how often he had said or done things just for her.

"Are you well?" Kitty, who was sitting to her left, whispered.

Mary shook her head. "I have been a monstrous fool."

"How so?"

"It matters not," Mary assured her.

"Are you certain?"

Mary smiled reassuringly at her younger sister.

"I am positive. I shall be well." Eventually. Most likely. She hoped. However, her heart was still racing with fear, growing more boisterous in its anxious state as an idea grasped her mind. Steadying herself with a slowly exhaled breath, she swallowed the last of her wine and, as she rose to follow Lady Matlock from the room, caught Lydia's shawl and gave it a soft tug.

"What is it?" Lydia asked.

Mary drew her to the side and slowed so that they fell behind their sisters and Lady Matlock. When the others were far enough removed, Mary lowered her voice and said, "Do you remember where Sally's is?"

"Why?" Lydia asked cautiously.

"I need to go there."

"Why?" Lydia asked again in the same concerned tone.

"I have not lost my mind," Mary assured her. Her heart was likely gone, but not her mind. "There is something I must know."

"And you must discover it at Sally's?"

"Yes. Do you remember where it is?"

Lydia shook her head. "I am deplorable with directions."

That was true.

"But," Lydia whispered, "I am certain the colonel would know the way."

"Do you think he would take us there?" It was a scandalous proposition. She should not even ask. She should withdraw the idea now, but she could not. She needed to know when Lord Westonbury had severed his relationship with his mistress.

"Perhaps. I will ask him." Lydia leaned closer to Mary. "Does this have to do with his brother?"

Mary nodded.

"Do you love him?"

Mary shrugged and then nodded. "I think I do." She more than just thought she knew, but she was not yet ready to admit such a thing outside of the safe confines of her mind.

Lydia squealed softly and embraced her. "I will persuade him to take us."

A moment of joy followed very closely by a nearly overwhelming sense of stupidity overtook Mary. She was mad to be proposing a visit to a brothel. Perhaps it was not just her heart that was lost but also her mind.

And, later, when she and Lydia told the colonel

of the scheme, he seemed to agree that Mary had lost her mind.

"Please," Lydia begged. "Sally is a very nice lady."

"It is a brothel." The colonel's features were hard.

"You are correct. It was a stupid idea," Mary agreed. "I am certain there are better ways to discover if your brother has truly given up his mistress."

"You could ask him," Colonel Fitzwilliam suggested.

"Except he is not here." It was growing quite late and still, Lord Westonbury had not returned to Matlock House. She looked down at her hands. "What is it like there?"

"Why do you ask?"

Why must everyone keep inquiring about why she said things tonight? Why could they not just simply answer her questions or accept her statements without knowing her motive for saying them?

Mary shrugged. "I was curious is all."

"I have been no further than Sally's apartment

when Darcy and I were there to collect your sisters."

"Was it a clean house?"

"The parts I saw were."

"Did you see any of the... um... er..."

"Ladies?"

Mary's cheeks burned as she nodded.

"No. Why?"

"I wondered if they looked... well... um... healthy."

"Ah." Colonel Fitzwilliam nodded. "That is not an unworthy curiosity." He sat silently for a moment with his bad eye closed while he studied her with his good eye. Then, blowing out a breath, he shook his head. "My mother will likely kill me for this if she finds out."

"Are we going?" Lydia asked eagerly.

"Only if we can do it in such a fashion that your faces are concealed. I should hate to be the cause of social ruin for either of you."

Chapter 18

Wes watched port swirled up the sides of his glass and then down. When it had stopped moving, he took a sip and then swirled it again.

He was not good enough.

He shook his head as the discomposing thought washed over him. He had a title. He had a fortune. He was not a bad-looking fellow. He was amiable. He was what every marriage-minded miss and her mother wanted in a prize catch. He had heard it whispered by more than one matron, so he knew he was not puffing himself up without just cause.

And yet, to the one person whose opinion mattered most to him, all he possessed was not enough. She demanded more.

He sighed.

She deserved more. She was not just another pretty face in a light-coloured gown, lining the walls with the other hopeful debutants waiting, eagerly, to be selected by the likes of him. No, Mary was more than that. She knew her mind. She knew what she wanted. And she was not going to be swayed by all the charm, money, or titles in the world to give up that which she held to as important. She was the prettiest immovable force he had ever met.

He blew out a breath and took another sip of his port. As much as he wanted to drain the contents of the carafe beside him before burying his foxed mind and body beneath the blankets on his bed here at Brook Street, he could not. Feeling sorry for himself was not going to win Mary for him. Nor was being satisfied and self-righteous about who he was. He might be the Viscount Westonbury, heir of the body of the Earl of Matlock, but that did not exempt him from being an honorable gentleman.

He placed his empty glass on his desk and rose from his chair.

He would have his belongings returned from Matlock House tomorrow. He could do without them for one night. What he could not do without, however, was Mary, and therefore, he could not and would not give up his fight to persuade her to consider him. He had to find some way to prove to her that he cared about the things which she held close to her heart – respect, love, and a conscious-ness that everyone around her was a person with great potential.

He turned back at the door and surveyed his study.

Had she not declared his potential to her cousins? She thought he was capable of being both a man of privilege and duty. Again, he considered how pleased his mother would be by such a thing. It was, after all, what both she and his father had attempted to tell him in their own ways. He would not disappoint any of them further than he had.

He shook his head. What a self-indulgent being he had become! Until this moment, he had not considered his seeking amusement to be a disap-pointment. He had only ever considered how it gratified his desires.

However, his greatest desire had just hours ago told him that he was not to be the recipient of her pleasures. Her smiles, her teases, her scowls, and her lectures would not be his alone. She was saving them for someone who saw beyond himself. And in that – he blew out a breath as the thought hit him squarely – he had been the cause of his own disappointment.

It was not a permanent disappointment. It could not be. He would not allow it to be, for he would pour every ounce of himself into becoming a gentleman who might be given the opportunity to win Miss Mary Bennet. There would never again be a need for his mother to bar him from his home.

His eyebrows rose, and his mouth popped open. That was it! He would begin with Clarice.

He pulled open the door to this study.

"My horse. I need my horse made ready immediately," he called to his butler before taking the stairs two at a time. He could not show up at Sally's in his robe and slippers. A proper suit of clothes was what he needed. He was visiting Clarice as a friend and on business – not for any other purpose or to participate in the usual sorts of things he did when he called on her. This time, they would sit in chairs, fully clothed, and he would listen to her as she talked – if she was both available and willing to talk to him that is.

He rubbed his chin.

She might be otherwise engaged. She had been

his exclusively – save for when he had sent Langley to see her – but he had closed his account and severed their arrangement the morning after he had seen his actions through the eyes of Mrs. Salter's words at that ball. Still, he must take the chance that she would be willing to see him for his ability to win Mary depended upon it.

~*~*~

No more than three-quarters of an hour later, Wes was standing inside Sally's establishment, considering that this was perhaps the soberest he had ever been when here.

Had the drawing room always smelled so strongly of liquor and cigars? The aroma reminded him quite sharply of his club. He perched on the edge of a chair as he waited to discover if he would be granted access to Clarice.

"My lord," Sally said as she entered the room.

Wes sprang to his feet.

"I was not expecting to see you again," Sally continued.

"I did not expect to return," Wes acknowledged. "However, there is a matter with which I think Clarice can be of service." He straightened the sleeve of his jacket. He was nervous? That was foolish. There was no need to be nervous. He had been here numerous times, although, he had to admit, it had never been for the reason he was here now.

"That is why my house is here, my lord, to provide service to gentlemen such as yourself."

Wes shook his head. "I am not looking for that sort of service."

Sally's left eyebrow rose in question.

"It has been brought to my attention that young women such as Clarice often turn to providing services such as your establishment does for reasons that are beyond their control." He shrugged. "This is likely a poor way to discover what I need to know, but I was hoping I might ask Clarice to tell me more about how she came to be here."

"And why do you need to know this?"

The image of a stern but beautiful young lady came to mind, and Wes smiled. "It has also been brought to my attention that I am a lord and with my title comes a responsibility to all those who live in England."

Sally looked amused.

"And..." Wes's heart was racing. How he hoped no one would walk in on this discussion. He was certain that he would become the source of many a good jest if another gentleman was to hear him right now.

"And?" Sally echoed when Wes paused.

"And this person who had informed me of these things is particularly concerned about the plight of disadvantaged females."

Sally's eyes were fairly dancing with mirth. "And does this young lady have a name?"

"I am not certain she would want me to share it here," Wes replied.

Sally chuckled. "I would imagine she would not. So, is this young lady the reason for your termination of our business arrangement?"

"Yes."

"A future Lady Westonbury?" Sally pressed.

"If I can ever persuade her to have me."

Again, Sally chuckled. "Is she not swayed by your title, my lord?"

"Not a whit."

"Years ago, I met a young woman who was determined to marry only a gentleman with good and honorable intentions. She was delightful, and I have lately come to learn she succeeded in her quest." She motioned for Wes to follow her as a gentleman of about fifty years of age entered the drawing room.

"Sir." Sally greeted him with a nod of her head. "I am certain that Clarice will be happy to be of service." She waved at the stairs. "You know the way." She winked. "And I'll not even charge you for your time."

Wes chuckled, thanked her, and scooted up the stairs. Two crates stood one atop the other in the hallway next to Clarice's open door.

"Are you going on a journey?" Wes asked when he entered her room.

"I am." Clarice, dressed in a simple blue gown with a cap on her head, stood on a stool, pulling things from the shelf in her wardrobe. "One from which I am not returning." She stepped down from her perch and placed the things she held in an open trunk on her bed. "I was not expecting you, but if you will give me a moment to change –"

"I am not here for sex."

Clarice turned slowly from her trunk to face him. "You are not?"

Wes shook his head. "I was hoping you could tell me somewhat about yourself and how you came to be here."

A furrow formed between her dark brown eyes. "Why? I am not looking for a suitor, my lord. If I have given you any indication that I might care for you beyond how one cares for a friend, I must apologize."

Wes shook his head. "I love Mary."

Clarice blinked.

"I met her when I went to see that my brother was still living."

"And is he?"

"Yes, yes. He is, though he was severely injured and may never have the full use of one of his eyes again, but he is, thankfully, living. In fact, he is going to be getting married as soon as his lady and my mother are satisfied that he has recovered enough."

"That is excellent news." She motioned to the two chairs near her hearth. When he was seated, she took her seat. "May I ask why you wish to know about me if you love another?"

Wes settled back into his chair and contemplated how best to answer that.

"You look besotted," Clarice said with a small giggle.

"I am completely lost to her, Clarice. She is not

like any lady I have ever met before." He leaned forward, his attention fully focused on explaining Mary to Clarice. "She is demanding. She scolds and scowls – quite prettily, I must say – but her heart is good. She cares so deeply for so many things." He exhaled. How he longed to be one of the things about which Mary was passionate.

"She scolds you?" Clarice sounded flabbergasted by the thought.

Wes nodded. "Most severely when we first met, though less so now. It does not matter to her that I have a title. She still expects me to be honorable."

"Indeed?"

Again, Wes nodded. "She equates my having had a mistress with a lack of respect for women. Of course, that also has something to do with the fact that I offered to pay her sisters for kisses when I first met them – however, in my defense, I did not know they were her sisters. I did not even know who she was at that time."

Clarice smiled as tears glistened in her eyes. "I think I would like her."

"You would?" Wes asked in surprise. He could not conceive how what he had shared about Mary would move Clarice to tears.

Clarice nodded. "It was a hatred for gentlemen who disrespect ladies which brought me here."

Wes gaped. How...?

"I know the two do not seem to mesh, my lord, but here, I know the sorts of men I might see. They are here to be pleasured no matter who might be waiting for them at home. I know what is expected of me when a gentleman arrives at my door." She sighed. "I could have become a governess or a maid or some other such thing rather than a courtesan, but I have seen how some men expect more than a cleaned room or a child's instruction from girls in their employ." Her expression grew sad. "And I know the look of pain on the lady's face when she discovers her husband has begun dallying with others." She shook her head. "I know that my thinking is not without its flaws, but to me, it seemed that being a lady of the night for a time was the best way to retain my power."

"Do you hate me?"

She shook her head. "You do not have a wife and children at home. Again, I know that some would condemn me for my thoughts."

"But if I had a wife and children, you would loathe me?"

"It would make it more challenging to take you to bed if you did."

Wes sank back in his chair. "I assume there are reasons for all of this."

Clarice nodded and looked away. "My father. My uncle. Several of my father's friends. Even the gentleman to whom my father tried to betroth me."

"Will you tell me about it? I need to know if there is any way I can help better the lives of women."

"For her? For Mary?"

"Yes. Please. I do not wish to live without her."

Clarice smiled. "And you are done with places such as this?"

"Forever."

"Very well, if that is the case, then I will tell you."

For the next hour, Wes listened and questioned as Clarice told of a father who visited courtesans and carried home disease to his wife and several maids. She told him about how her uncle paid her cousin's governess to take a concoction to dispose of a suspected by-blow. She was not supposed to know about that, but she had discovered it when her father was entertaining, and she had overheard a conversation around a billiard table. The gentleman, who her father had been promoting to her, was a member of that party and had joined in the general laughter over the governess being indisposed for several weeks and in need of persuasion to continue her clandestine meetings with her employer.

All in all, by the end of the hour, Wes as disgusted with the behaviour of some men as Clarice was. None of the stories were particularly shocking or out of the ordinary, but when told altogether and seen through the eyes of a woman, they took on a new shade – one which was not at all of a pleasing colour.

When their discussion drew to an end, Wes rose. "I thank you for opening my understanding. I am not certain what can be done, but I now understand the need."

Clarice extended her hand to him. "I wish you good fortune and joy with Mary."

Wes moved toward the door, and Clarice followed.

"I need to see Sally about something," she explained when he looked back at her.

"Where are you going?" he asked while they descended the steps.

"I cannot say. However, I will tell you that I have always wished to have a tearoom, and your generous gift has provided what I need to make a go of it."

"I wish you prosperity."

They had just reached the bottom of the stairs when the door before them opened, and the lady who entered gasped.

"Mary!" Wes cried as he flew to her when she stumbled backward at seeing him.

Chapter 19

Mary wrung her hands as she sat in the carriage. "This is a very bad idea."

"It is not the best. I will give you that," Colonel Fitzwilliam agreed. "It could go very wrong, but I think it is also necessary."

"You do?" Mary turned from looking out the small window on the side of their hired conveyance.

"I can appreciate your need to know about Sally's."

"You can?" Lydia asked in surprise. "Is it more than mere curiosity?"

Colonel Fitzwilliam nodded. "I believe so. You see, I would want to know the lay of the land before entering a skirmish. To that end, I would send out scouts or attempt to discover intelligence on my own before making a decision about the engagement of my men. I am not the sort who is willing to toss away my own life or those of my men on the impulse of a moment." He looked at Mary but spoke to Lydia. "Your sister wishes to know if this is a battle she has a hope of winning, before deciding to put forward her plan to claim the land."

"I am not fighting a battle." Mary turned back toward the window. It was not terribly bright inside the carriage as little light was filtering in from the lamps outside, but it was still uncomfortable to be looked at so intently as Colonel Fitzwilliam was looking at her. It felt as if he could read her inner thoughts.

"Yes, you are."

"I do not understand," Lydia said softly.

"What does Miss Mary believe about men having mistresses?" the colonel replied.

"They should not have them," Mary answered.

"But why? And do not quote me what a parson would say. I want to know why Miss Mary says a gentleman should not have a mistress."

"I would rather not discuss this." Her insides were twisted in enough knots without having to rehearse her views on such topics – views which she knew were not popular with everyone in society.

"I would say..."

Apparently, not wishing to discuss it was not going to stop Lydia from doing so.

"She finds it disrespectful."

Mary peeked at her sister and saw Colonel Fitzwilliam nodding.

"She is not wrong. A gentleman who takes a mistress does break his vows to his wife." He held up a finger. "But Wes is not yet married."

"Is it so wrong to want a husband who has loved only me in the way he loves a wife?" Mary asked.

"Oh, you did say that!" Lydia cried. "I remember it very well."

"No, it is not wrong," the colonel answered. "But is it wrong to turn away a potential mate because of an error in his past?"

"No," Lydia answered before Mary could form a word, "if he has never changed his ways, it would be best to send him on his way."

"Precisely. And that is the battle Miss Mary is fighting. Wes has loved others as one would love a wife. Miss Mary needs to know if it was just an error of the past or one which speaks to a lifelong deficit." He shook his head. "It is not an easy thing to give up one's hopes and claim a new reality. It takes time and struggle to find the way to making peace with it."

He touched his eye, and Mary understood that he knew very well the struggle which was raging in her mind. Lord Westonbury was so very far from the sort of gentleman Mary had ever dreamt of marrying. She had always imagined herself married to a gentleman with a small estate, who never ventured very far into society and was content to be at home with his family. She smiled to herself. She had always thought she would marry someone a good bit like her father, and Lord Westonbury was not at all like her father.

"We are here."

Mary grabbed Colonel Fitzwilliam's arm when he moved to open the door. "We should just go back home."

"No, Miss Mary, I did not sneak you down the servants' stairs, out the back door, down the alley, and around the corner to hale a hack only to have you back out now. You know as well as I do that you need to do this. Even if all you do is set foot inside the door and see that it is not so very different from an inn, you need to put a real picture in your mind to replace the one it might have concocted."

How did he know she had imagined how a brothel might look?

"Are you ready? We will be right beside you."

"Sally is very nice," Lydia encouraged.

Mary drew in a shaky breath and exhaled it slowly. Her insides had never quivered as much as they were right now, but she knew what Colonel Fitzwilliam said was true. She needed to see this place for herself. She nodded. "I think I am."

"We will be beside you," the colonel assured her once again before climbing out of the carriage and assisting her and Lydia.

Mary stood for a moment in front of Sally's establishment. It looked very much like a lot of houses in this part of town looked. If one did not know that this was a brothel, one would pass it by without a second thought. There was a knocker on the door, just as there was anywhere else, and there was a man in livery to answer when one did knock. It all seemed so ordinary and respectable.

Until she stepped inside.

There, coming down the stairs and conducting a

conversation with a rather attractive young woman was Lord Westonbury.

She gasped and stepped backward. This had been a very bad idea. She should not have come. Pain welled in her chest and sent tears to her eyes. She needed to leave.

"Mary!" Lord Westonbury caught her by the arm.

"Unhand me!"

"No."

"I am not going to swoon." She attempted to pull away from him. "I wish to leave."

"Then I will go with you."

"No. Please. Leave me alone." She did not wish to have anyone with her right now. She wanted to be miserable and angry without an audience.

"I cannot."

"What is all this disturbance?"

A lady of many years stepped out from the door on the right side of the corridor.

"We do not argue and fight here. It is not that sort of place. I will have to ask you..." She stopped speaking suddenly as she took in who was standing before her. "Miss Lydia?"

Lydia bobbed her head up and down, stepping

forward to greet Sally. "My sister was curious about your establishment," she added to her greeting in a not altogether discreet whisper.

"Your sister?" A smile spread across the older woman's face. "Please, come into my home." She moved to the door through which she had entered the corridor just moments before.

"Is this not all your home?" Mary asked.

"Oh, no. I own the building, of course, and I see to its management. However, this apartment is my home. The other apartments are leased to others."

"Ladies of the night?" Mary pressed her lips together. She was angry, and she did not approve of brothels, but those facts did not give her the right to sound so disapproving. The woman had just offered to accept them into her private home.

"Yes," Sally replied. "Not everyone approves. I am under no assumption that they do." She motioned to her home once again.

"I would rather return home," Mary said softly.

"It does not appear as if Lord Westonbury is willing to allow that to happen."

Mary scowled at Lord Westonbury. She wanted to say that she did not care what Lord Westonbury wanted or thought, but she could not. Her rebellious heart cared very much about both of those things.

"Please," he begged. "I am not here for the reason you think."

"That is very likely true," Sally said. "My lord severed his relationship with me some time ago. Not that he had been a visitor here for some time before that." Sally held Mary's gaze. "I do not lie about such things. Not for any amount of money. A wife deserves the truth."

"I am not his wife."

Sally smiled. "Not yet." Then, she stepped into her apartment, and Mary, rather unwillingly but filled with curiosity, followed.

"What did you tell her?" she hissed to Lord Westonbury, who ignored her question.

"Miss Mary, this is Cla—"

"Hannah," the pretty young woman said. "It is the name my mother gave me," she explained to Lord Westonbury who was looking rather startled. "Clarice is the name I gave myself when I chose to leave my father's house."

Mary was aware that she was moving and being seated, but only just. Had Lord Westonbury just introduced her to his mistress? And had that lady just said she had decided to leave her father's house?

"Clarice is..."

"Please do not tell me," Mary whispered.

"My former mistress." He had ignored her once again! "Former," he repeated. "As in *before* I met you."

He pressed a handkerchief into her hand. "Oh, my love, I am so sorry," he whispered. "I did not mean to hurt you. I never would. Well, that is not entirely true," he smiled sheepishly. "I would not purposefully hurt you. I might out of ignorance."

Mary's quivering lips tipped up into a small smile. Even now, he was being honest with her.

"Which it appears I have done." He was kneeling before her and held one of her hands.

"Why are you here?" The colonel did not sound at all pleased with his brother.

"I could ask the same of you," Lord Westonbury replied.

"Gentlemen," Sally interrupted. "I will have no fisticuffs. Lord Westonbury, I believe you were asked a question first."

"Miss Mary once accused me of not knowing any of the women in this establishment, so I am here to rectify that by learning about one. The one who I have spent a great deal of time with over the past year and a half." He grimaced at Mary. "Again, I apologize for the pain that hearing such a thing might cause you. But a lord learns. About society. And then, a lord uses that knowledge to help make decisions which will improve England." He shrugged. "I was learning. It was not a pleasant lesson. Some gentlemen can be absolute arses."

A small laugh escaped Mary before she could catch it.

"That they can be," Sally agreed. "Now, Colonel, I believe it is your turn to answer."

"Miss Lydia could not remember the way to Sally's house, so it seemed best if I kept her and Miss Mary from getting lost."

"Are you?" Sally motioned between the colonel and Lydia.

"We are betrothed but not officially," Lydia replied in a loud whisper. "He must heal some more before we can plan our future."

Sally nodded. "I had heard you were injured, and I do not recall you having a scar the last time you were here. I am happy you are doing so well, sir." She shook her head. "My, my, Fanny Gardiner's girls have done very well for themselves, have they not?"

"My sister Elizabeth is now Mrs. Darcy," Lydia informed Sally as if speaking to a good friend she had not seen in years, "and Jane is Mrs. Bingley."

"And you will be Mrs. Fitzwilliam, and, if my lord has his way, your sister will be his lady."

Lydia's head bobbed up and down. "That is what we hope."

"*We* hope?" Mary asked. "Are you including me in that? For I am not certain at this moment that you should."

"Oh, no!" Lydia cried. "I was not speaking for you." She pressed her lips together.

"Then who is *we*?"

Lydia shook her head. "I cannot say. I have promised."

"My money is on my mother," Wes muttered.

Lydia merely smiled and batted her lashes.

Sally chuckled. "Now, Miss Lydia, why did you need to find my house?"

"For Mary, of course."

Sally's face did not register that the *of course* was self-evident. However, that was how Lydia's mind worked at times. She just expected everyone to think as she did and understand everything she understood. But often, the only one who understood Lydia was Lydia – and occasionally, their mother.

"I was curious about your establishment," Mary swallowed, "and Lord Westonbury's relationship to it after what he said to Mrs. Salter."

"I have no idea what was said to Mrs. Salter or even who she is –"

"Nor do you wish to know who she is!" Lydia inserted. "She is vile."

"I will keep that in mind," Sally assured her. "As I was saying, I can clarify that Lord Westonbury has no current relationship with my establishment or any of the ladies who live here other than to be formerly acquainted." She looked at Clarice or Hannah – Mary was not sure which name would be best to think of that lady as. Hannah might be better as that was not the name Lord Westonbury would have used to address the woman. "I am not mistaken, am I?"

"No, not at all," Hannah assured Sally.

"What else would you like to know, my dear?" Sally asked Mary.

Mary looked around at all the faces of her companions. "Well," she began, but then paused.

The colonel nodded his encouragement to continue.

"I wanted to see if your establishment was clean, and that, well, that Hannah looked... healthy."

"Ah. I see. And what is your assessment?"

"Your establishment looks respectable. If I did not know what it was, I might mistake it for a well-cared-for boarding house." She glanced at Hannah. "And Hannah appears healthy."

"I am," Hannah assured her.

"You are certain?"

"As certain as I can be."

Well, that was a small comfort. She pulled her lip between her teeth. There was one other thing she wished to know.

"What is it?" Hannah encouraged.

"There are no children?" Oh, her cheeks must be brilliantly red for they were painfully warm.

"No, there are not. Nor will there be."

Mary nodded. That was good to know, was it not?

"I am leaving town tomorrow, and I am not returning," Hannah added. "Sally has been good to me, as had Lord Westonbury." She dropped her gaze as she said it. "And I have finally saved the funds I need to pursue what I truly wish to do." She looked up at Mary again. "And it is not to be a mistress – to anyone."

"But you chose to be one up until now?"

"Yes," Hannah answered. "My home was not a happy one, and while I attempted another line of employment before this, it paid little and demanded a great deal of effort to earn that money." She shrugged. "So, when I heard about Sally's, I came to meet her and decided to stay." She smiled. "I know that is hard to understand. My mother would not be pleased to know I had worked here, but it seemed the best option."

"Is there anything else you wish to know?" Sally asked.

"Not at the moment," Mary said. "Or, at least, not from you." Her mind was struggling to comprehend all she had heard so far.

"Ah. Well, I would offer you a private room to discuss whatever else needs to be discussed with Lord Westonbury. However, the only one which might be available is Clarice's room, and well, that seems a bit uncomfortable.

Indeed, it did! Meeting Lord Westonbury's mistress was bad enough. Mary had no desire to see where he had...well... she had no desire to even contemplate it.

"You are leaving tomorrow?"

Hannah nodded. "I cannot say where I am to go, or what name I might assume. There are those who would not give a woman like myself a chance to be successful if they knew I had worked in a brothel. In fact, there are those who would hear it and expect me to provide a service for them to keep the information secret."

"That is unfortunate," Lydia said, turning toward Mary. "Is that not similar to what we spoke about in the carriage? Whether people should be forever rejected for the deeds in their past?"

"It is very similar," the colonel assured her, which earned him a brilliant smile.

Mary turned her attention back to the gentleman who still knelt at her feet. To keep condemning him for his past was not right. Grace, mercy, and pardon were part of her duty to others, and acceptance, her heart cried. This time, she would not deny him if he wished for more than friendship.

"You never returned to Matlock House," she said.

"I am moving back to Brook Street since I am well."

"Only because you are well?" Or was it because of her?

He shrugged. "No."

She smiled. "You could call on me if you wished."

"As a friend?"

Mary could see the longing in his expression, and it echoed the beat of her heart. "If that is what you want," she replied.

"And if I wanted more?" There was a hopeful note to the question.

She cupped his cheek with the hand he was not holding. "In that case, I must insist that you call on me."

He blinked and stared at her blankly for a moment before a beautiful smile split his face. "Truly? You would welcome me as a suitor?"

"Yes." The word was no sooner out of her mouth than he was kissing her hand, and then rising to pull her into his embrace.

"My lord," Mary scolded, for it seemed the

proper thing to do when unexpectedly hugged in the presence of others. "I am only agreeing to let you call on me. I am making no other promises."

He released her but only enough to look down at her.

She scowled at him.

He arched a challenging eyebrow.

"At least not yet," she whispered.

He laughed, and, while still holding her with one arm, dug in his pocket with his other hand. Finding what he sought, he held up two half-crowns.

Her eyes grew wide, and she shook her head but just barely while he extended the money to Lydia. He was going to kiss her. Here, in an apartment of a brothel. She should push him away. She should scold him and tell him to stop. She should do something! However, she did not do any of the things she should do. Instead, she allowed, and even welcomed, him to claim her lips in a kiss which would do nothing to help her refuse him, but everything to lodge a permanent longing for him in her heart.

Chapter 20

Using the tip of his walking stick, Wes lifted the knocker on the door of Matlock House and let it fall. He drew in a deep breath and released it. What a glorious day it was! The clouds were gathering overhead, and the wind was unwelcoming, but he did not care. In his world, sunshine was peeking through the clouds which had hung over him for the last many weeks. Soon, all those little puffs of uncertainty and possible despair would be a long-forgotten memory. He had been given a chance to make Mary his. She had asked him to call on her, and she had allowed him to kiss her.

He closed his eyes and remembered her – the way she felt in his arms, the look of terror on her face when he produced his coins, the taste of her lips, the way she willingly gave herself to him, and the way she had nearly undone him. When was the last time he had ever felt his knees go wobbly at a kiss?

"My lord?"

Wes opened one eye. The expression of concern on Nibley's face only deepened Wes's joy. He doffed his hat and handed it along with his walking stick to the butler. "I am to be married," he announced.

"Indeed?" There was no small amount of surprise in the man's voice.

"Eventually." Wes allowed Nibley to take his coat. "I only have to finish convincing the young lady to accept me."

Nibley's lips twitched. "I am sure that will be easily done. You are a charming rascal."

"That I am," Wes agreed. "However, being allowed to call on her has taken a great deal of work on my part. Not that the improvement to my character was not needed. It was just not easily done." He straightened his coat sleeves. "But then, a treasure is not easily won, is it?"

"I should think not, my lord."

"In which room will I find my treasure?"

"I beg your pardon, my lord?"

"Miss Mary. Where might she be?"

If Matlock's long-time butler's lips had not twitched, Wes might have believed the surprise in his tone when he said, "Miss Mary, my lord?"

"Yes, Miss Mary." Wes cocked an eyebrow. "No one sneaks out of Matlock House without your knowledge. I dare say you knew perfectly well that I was here for her."

"I really could not say, my lord."

"Or should not," Wes muttered with a laugh. "Now, where is the lady?"

"She and your mother are awaiting you in the green drawing room. Do you wish to be announced?"

Wes opened his mouth to say no, then closed it. Being announced could be entertaining. He grimaced and shook his head. "No, not this time. I do not have a title prepared." He would have to craft a fitting announcement for when he called on Mary.

Though there was to be no announcement needed and Wes knew the way to the green drawing room, Nibley still led the way and upon opening the door to the room, announced, "Miss Mary, your young man, my lord, is here to see you."

Wes clapped the butler on the shoulder. "I quite like that title."

"You have not come to see me?" his mother said as he entered the room.

"No, not at all. If there is something to which you needed to attend, you may." He crossed the room, caught her face between his hands and kissed her forehead.

"You are incorrigible," she scolded with a smile.

"So you have told me before," he replied.

She held out her hand to him. "Help me out of this chair."

"Have your knees gone gouty?" he teased.

"Do you wish me to leave or not?"

He took her hand and helped her rise. She kept his hand for a moment after rising. "I know how troublesome you can be. Treat her with respect. I wish for grandchildren but not before the wedding."

"My lady!" Mary cried.

"You, I trust. It is my son whom I doubt."

"We would both have to misbehave for there to be grandchildren," Wes said.

Lady Matlock laughed. "I am quite aware of that. I have had two children, after all." She patted his cheek. "I did not think you still blushed, Reginald."

"Mother."

"Do not forget that I can be as trying as you," she warned. "The door will remain open, and Miss Mary only needs to ring, and someone will fly to her aid."

"Fly to her aid? Mother, what do you think I am?"

His mother grew quite serious. "You are as much your father's son as you are mine. I know how young love and a charming gentleman can sway even the most staid lady toward impropriety." She smiled. "I have not always been old." She proceeded to leave the room but stopped at the door. "Just to clarify. I will hold you responsible for any mischief, Reginald." She shook her head. "But I am very happy to see you here." She sighed. "Very happy." She gave Mary an encouraging nod and was gone.

What was that nod about? "You have not changed your mind, have you?"

"About what, my lord?"

"Allowing me to call on you."

Mary shook her head and looked excessively confused.

"It seemed my mother was prompting you to tell

me something unpleasant." He unbuttoned his coat and sat down next to her on the settee. He watched her duck her head ever so slightly as she lowered her eyes. "You are going to tell me something unpleasant."

"No, no. I am not." She paused, took three deep breaths, and looked at him. "I was discussing something with your mother."

In the whole expanse of his life, nothing good had ever followed those words, and his heart immediately began to beat a bit faster.

"You scare me, and your mother thinks it is best that we clear the air in regard to that before we proceed."

"I am sorry. Did you say I frighten you?" That did not sound promising for a happy future.

"Yes."

Wes sank backward. "How so?"

She watched herself twist her fingers in her lap instead of looking at him. "I was never supposed to fall in love with someone like you."

"But you have fallen in love with me?" That bit sounded hopeful.

She peeked up at him and smiled. "Against my

better judgment, I have fallen completely and utterly in love with you and that scares me."

"Let me see if I have this correct. You are terrified both by me and by loving me?" He covered her hands so that her fingers would stop nervously twisting.

"Yes." She sighed. "This is not easily admitted."

"I will not tease you."

"I know you will not, but it is still not easy."

He lifted her fingers to her lips. "Tell me, why does loving me scare you?" It would likely be easier to hear her say something about that than about his person, so it seemed the best place to start.

"Do you think your mother would believe me if I said I told you but did not?"

Wes chuckled. "No. I have tried something similar. She is unnaturally good at deciphering when someone is telling her the truth or not. Tell me."

Mary straightened her shoulders. "Then, it is best to just come to the point, I suppose, and be done with it."

That did sound a good deal like something Mary would do.

"I do not want to be hurt. If you should tire of

me, I would die – not physically, but my heart would."

"Tire of you? Why should I ever tire of you?"

Mary shrugged. "I am not..."

"You are not like any other woman that I have ever met," he supplied. "But that is not a bad thing. That is a very, very good thing."

"It is?"

He nodded.

"I can be so critical."

"And I can be challenging."

"That is true."

He chuckled. "We will argue."

"I imagine we will since we do now." She sighed. "It is more than just our tendency to knock heads." Pink stained her cheeks. "You may discover that I am not as... interesting as your wife as someone else might be." She leaned toward him and lowered her voice when he did not respond. "In my wifely duties."

"I do not care if you never throw a dinner party or host a soiree, and I would rather that you refrain from being too creative with the household accounts or servants under your purview."

She gave an exasperated huff. "That is not what I meant."

"The marriage bed is not a duty," he whispered. "No matter what you might have been told in an effort to make marital relations sound unpleasant, they are not. They are to be enjoyed by both the husband and the wife."

"Your mother said something similar, but I have never done... that, and you have. What if I am not as pleasing as Clarice? She is very pretty. What if I cannot do what she did how she did it?"

He wanted to reassure her immediately, but she did not look as if she was finished speaking. Therefore, he placed his tongue between his teeth and waited.

"Look at me. I am nothing special. I am not lively like Lydia or Elizabeth. I am not naturally sweet like Jane or Kitty, and, compared to my sisters or Clarice, I am plain. I have plain features, plain eyes, and plain hair. My accomplishments are tolerable, but not exemplary. The only thing at which I excel is scolding and lecturing. I have no connections of any value and no fortune." She looked at the hand he held. "And I have not treated you as I should have."

His tongue would be contained no longer. "You placed a picture of what I should be in front of me. I do not see how that is not treating me with the greatest respect one could give."

"I should have been willing to forgive you for how you treated my sisters long before I did."

"But do you not see that it was your willingness to lay my sin before me that has made me love you more?"

She shook her head.

He caught her face in his hands and kissed her gently, the sweetness of being allowed such a precious privilege as to kiss her welling up and threatening to overwhelm him, before resting his forehead on hers. "I love you. I desire only you." He took her hands and sat back again. "I want you to tell me when I am being a fool. Do you realize how very few dare to disagree with a viscount? Most will do whatever they need to do to keep a connection to me and my father, but the people who truly care for me – my mother, my father, Darcy, Richard, Langley — they all call me out when I have gone astray. *I* matter more to them than my title does." He lifted her fingers to his lips. How fortunate he was to have found a woman like her, a lady who saw *him*.

"I cannot undo the past. I have experienced things which you have not, and I know you do not approve of such behaviour." He placed a finger on her lips to keep her from speaking. "I am learning that what is permissible is not always wise and that a fleeting moment of pleasure can have far-reaching consequences outside of myself." He had seen those consequences in her eyes last night when she saw him at Sally's and again just now. "I promise you, Mary, that a kiss has never been so stirring as the one you allowed me last night or as sweet as the one you gave me just now. I have given my body to another before you, but I have never given my heart. That is only and always yours if you will have it and me." He slipped off the settee to kneel before her. "I know you only gave me permission to call on you, and I know I should likely be patient. However, I cannot be, and considering the topics we have canvassed, I dare to hope that I have a chance of being accepted."

She was smiling at him. This was good.

"Say you will marry me. Please. There is nothing I desire more in this world than to have you by my side, scolding me, for the rest of my life. I can ride to Longbourn tomorrow to speak to your father if you will but say yes."

"He will be excessively shocked that I would accept you and might not believe you."

"That is a possibility." A very great one.

She tipped her head and placed her hand on his cheek. "You could write to him and I could add my assurances."

"Does that mean you are agreeing to marry me?"

Was there a sweeter sound than her soft giggle?

"Yes, yes, I will marry you."

There was a sweeter sound, and that was it.

As she leaned forward and kissed him, brilliant sunshine flooded his existence while thunder rumbled outside. He captured her face when she broke the kiss and drew her to him again. However, only kissing her was not enough. He longed to feel her in his embrace again, and so, he rose and pulled her from her seat and into his arms. He held her tightly, enjoying the softness of her form against him, delighting in how she willingly leaned into him and wrapped her arms around his waist. He ran his hand up her back to the nape of her neck. He pulled back slightly. "My body, like my heart, is yours, my beautiful love. Never will either ever belong to another."

Tears sprang to her eyes, and her lower lip quivered as she whispered a thank you before he kissed her once again.

Chapter 21

Four weeks passed quite quickly.

There had been a journey to Longbourn to endure the raptures of Mrs. Bennet and receive permission to marry Mr. Bennet's middle daughter along with a proper lecture about staying his course of fidelity. It had surprised Wes to some extent that the gentleman had taken him to task so severely, but Wes could not fault him for it. In fact, he had jotted down a few notes in his journal that night so he might remember how to properly scold a prospective suitor for any daughter he might have.

Then, there had been several soirees in town at which to make his betrothal known – nights at the theatre, dinner parties, musicales. How he had delighted in introducing Mary as his betrothed! And he had, to his great pleasure, been allowed more than one dance with her at all the balls which they had attended.

She had taken drives with him in the park. She had taken tea with him at her aunt's house – with the children. She had sat with him to receive callers at Matlock House. She had worn pelisses and ball gowns and day dresses. She had even worn that pink dress she had worn to her first musicale just because he had asked her to do so. Strangely, he did not mind the cut of the neckline when he knew that she and the loveliness such a dress revealed were to be his.

She had shone at each and every event, but not as brightly as she did today, standing next to him, with her hand in his as he pledged his troth.

The rector turned from him to Mary and began his instruction to her regarding her vows.

"I, Mary Amelia Bennet," she repeated, "take thee, Reginald Arthur Fitzwilliam to my wedded husband." Mary glanced at the rector who prompted her with the next words. Her hand was trembling slightly in his. Wes squeezed her hand and was rewarded with a smile before she said the next words.

"To have and to hold, from this day forward."

She paused to take a breath. "For better or worse, for richer for poorer, in sickness and in health."

She once again paused to breath. She was nervous, but it was not because she was marrying him. Nor was it the size of the church and the crowd within it which had her trembling. She had confessed her trepidation over the service to him just yesterday, and he knew that she was not only repeating words and pledging herself to him, but she was also speaking to God.

The thought was enough to cause a small tremor to wobble his knees as well. Taking an oath before a parson or the woman one loved was a solemn thing and not to be taken lightly, but when he viewed it through Mary's eyes and imagined, as she did, God himself shining down through the stained-glass windows of the building, the gravity of the occasion grew exponentially.

"To love, cherish, and to obey," her eyebrow quirked slightly as she said the last word and Wes's lips twitched. Theirs would not a marriage without some discussions about whether this or that should be done, and he would not want it any other way. He valued her opinion for he valued her.

"Till death do us part, according to God's holy ordinance; and thereto I give thee my troth." She gave his hand a squeeze before releasing it.

Wes withdrew her ring from his pocket. It was no simple band of gold. It was a filigree emerald and diamond concoction with a large emerald in the middle surrounded by six diamonds – one at the top, one at the bottom, and two on each of the sides – with four smaller emeralds standing in pairs as sentries next to the double diamonds on both sides. Mary gasped softly when she saw it, for he had kept it a secret from her. He had only told her that it paled in value and beauty to her.

She looked up at him with misty eyes as he took her hand and repeated the words the rector spoke first.

"With this ring, I thee wed." He paused and held her gaze as he spoke the next words slowly and deliberately. "With my body I *thee* worship." She caught the corner of her bottom lip between her teeth. "And with all my worldly goods I thee endow. In the name of the Father, and of the Son, and of the Holy Ghost. Amen" He held the ring in place on her finger for a moment and mouthed an *I love you* before kneeling for prayer.

When the prayer, blessings, and singing were done, Wes tucked his wife's hand into the crook of his elbow and led her out of the St. George's.

"It is so beautiful," Mary said as she held out her hand and admired her ring in the barouche which would take them to Matlock House for the wedding feast.

"Not as beautiful as the lady who wears it." He leaned over and kissed her. "There is something engraved on the band." He took her hand and slipped the ring from her finger to show her. "It says 'I thee cherish. I thee worship.' I left out the with my body portion as it was getting rather long and if you decide to pass this on to a son or grandson that part might not be as welcome by whomever they wish to marry."

"Oh, Wes," she said as he returned the ring to its rightful place.

He cupped her smiling face in his hands. "I will never break a promise to you."

"I know."

"Do you truly?"

She nodded. "You have proven yourself to be quite trustworthy, my lord."

"And I intend to be always so where you are concerned, my lady. Now, I do not care if the top of the carriage is down, I fully intend to be utterly improper and kiss my bride several times on the way to our feast." And he did with nary a scold from his wife.

~*~*~

"A real lord is my son." Mrs. Bennet released Mary from a hug and shook her head. "And to be married at St. George's, by a common license, but still, it is an honour." She shook her head once again. "I must say I did not expect it to be my most sardonic daughter who would claim such an honour." She sighed. "You are so like your father." Then, she kissed Mary on the cheek and moved on so that others could greet the happy couple and express their joy on their marriage.

"My mother seems almost completely pleased," Mary muttered to Wes once all the guests had entered and they were free to roam.

"Yes, I fear I have disappointed her because I did not procure a special license."

"You most certainly have," Mary teased. "However, I do think having the wedding breakfast here with dancing and all will ease her disappointment."

"Do you wish to go in?" He nodded to the ballroom where the musicians were tuning their instruments and their guests were milling about.

She shook her head. "Not just yet. We are not required until the third dance. Your mother thought we might like a little time before we are presented."

"Then, where would you like to go?"

"The library?"

"That seems a very good place. It will be quiet and unoccupied unless Richard has already staked his claim."

"Your mother plans to announce his and Lydia's betrothal today."

Wes nodded. "She asked me if I minded sharing my joyous day with him."

"She asked me the same thing." Mary rested her head against his arm. "I am happy for them. I would never wish to be the cause of limiting their joy or that of my mother or father. Such an announcement with so many present to witness it will set Mama up for years."

Wes chuckled. "I can just hear her relating the tale now."

"I am glad I will be in town and not at Longbourn to hear it. Mama can be rather boisterous, as you well know."

"I do not mind her liveliness, though I will admit that even I find it overwhelming." He nodded to Richard who was walking down the hall with Lydia, followed by Darcy and Elizabeth, as well as Jane and Bingley. "I say it is good to see you, Bingley! Are you returning to Netherfield directly, or are you in town for a while?"

"We are in town until Caroline's wedding. Then, well, then, we have not decided what we are going to do. Darcy has invited us to join him at Pemberley, and we are almost entirely set on the idea. Are you going to Matlock?"

Wes nodded. "There is a cottage on the estate that I have asked to be made ready. Mother would have us under her roof, of course, but I should like to be my own man as much as I am allowed."

"A wise thing, that," Darcy agreed.

"Indeed," Bingley muttered, causing Wes's brows to rise.

"His mother-in-law might be too close for his comfort," Richard inserted.

"Ah, right. We were just speaking about that."

"Mrs. Bennet is a wonderful woman," Darcy said.

"Of course, she is," Bingley said. "I am not intimating that she is not. However, I should like to be a little further removed for Jane's comfort presently."

"Are you unwell?" Mary asked.

"Only at times," Jane answered with a smile and rested her hand on her abdomen.

"Oh! How lovely!" Mary cried. "Does Aunt Gardiner know?"

Jane nodded. "We have already discussed how close in age our children will be."

"You are going to have a baby?" Lydia asked in delight.

"I am," Jane replied.

"And are you, Lizzy?"

"Lydia!" Mary scolded. "One does not ask such a thing in company."

Lydia's eyes grew wide. "I apologize. I forgot there were so many of us here."

"I am not," Elizabeth answered. "But I am not disappointed by that," she assured Lydia when Lydia's expression fell.

Lydia's lips tipped upward, and she turned back to Jane. "Does Kitty know?"

"Not yet, nor does Mama." She said the last part quite sternly. "This is Mary's day and yours. There is plenty of time to share our news with Mama later."

"I will not say a thing," Lydia assured her.

To Wes, Mary did not look convinced that her youngest sister would not say something. They got on well enough, but the difference between the two sisters was great. Where Mary was serious and contemplative, Lydia was spontaneous and exuberant. However, such a personality seemed to mesh very well with his brothers, while Mary's balanced his own perfectly. He lifted her hand to his lips.

"Have you seen Kitty?" Lydia asked. "I had hoped to show her my new slippers. They do not match this dress, but they are absolutely adorable and must not go unseen for too long."

Wes chuckled. "We have not seen her."

"Nor have we," Bingley said.

"She was with Georgiana when last I saw her," Elizabeth said.

Down the hall, a cacophony of piano notes rang out.

"Perhaps they went to the music room," Richard suggested.

"It sounds as if that piece could use a great deal more practice," Bingley jested as he and Jane followed Lydia.

"Kitty!" Lydia cried from the doorway to the music room. "What are you doing?"

Wes and Mary hurried down the hall.

"Langley, what is the meaning of this," Darcy growled.

Good heavens! What had his friend done? Wes knew the answer as soon as he took in Miss Kitty's appearance. Her hair was dishevelled, and her lips appeared to have been most thoroughly kissed. Thankfully, her gown appeared to be in order.

"Could we refrain from shouting," Mary said, stepping into the room. "The incident is contained for now."

"That is wise thinking," Richard commended her. "Langley, take a seat away from Miss Bennet so that we might sort this out." The words were spoken as one might expect a seasoned colonel to bark out orders. "Lydia, see to Kitty."

"It is well in hand," Wes whispered, attempting to draw Mary toward the door. He would rather be kissing his wife than listening to Langley being lectured for kissing her sister.

"He is your friend," Mary whispered.

"Yes, but I do not control his actions."

"You might wish to save him from the actions of the other men in this room," Mary replied with a pointed look.

Wes scowled. "I am not so certain that I actually wish that."

"Did you see what they did to Wickham?"

Wes nodded. "I see your point. To have him arrive in the ballroom in such a state would cause some suspicion."

"Indeed," she said flatly.

"Well, Langley," Wes said, pushing his way to the forefront. "It appears we shall be brothers."

"Oh, I am not marrying him," Kitty said.

"I think the way you were allowing him to kiss you says otherwise," Lydia stepped up beside Wes, who looked at her in surprise. Perhaps she did share some traits with Mary, for she seemed to be very good at scolding.

"No one knows," Kitty said. "It was a mistake that will not happen again."

Wes watched Langley's jaw tighten. The kiss which had been interrupted was not a mistake to his friend.

"Oh, there you are," Lady Matlock joined them. "We have already had one set of dances." She stopped and looked from face to face, stopping when she saw Kitty. "Mr. Langley?" Her tone was stern. "Have you been kissing Miss Bennet?"

"He most certainly was when I opened the door," Lydia answered.

"Mr. Langley?" Lady Matlock said once again.

"Yes, my lady, I was."

"And have you presented your offer?"

"Kitty says she will not marry him," Lydia whispered.

"She gave up her right to decline when she allowed him to make such a mess of her hair." She turned to Miss Bennet. "I do hope it was only kissing which you allowed."

Kitty's eyes were wide as she nodded. Wes did not blame her. His mother was terrifying when she was put out.

"The only question is when the wedding should

take place, but I think that would be best discussed tomorrow." She patted Darcy's arm. "Or the following day. For now, Miss Lydia, please see to restoring your sister to her previous well-coiffured state, and Mr. Langley, you may take yourself downstairs."

Wes caught Langley by the arm. "What were you thinking?"

Langley nodded to the hall, and Wes followed him.

"I was thinking she welcomed my addresses and would be receptive of an offer at some point." Langley ran a hand through his hair. "I will leave. Call on me when you are able."

Wes knew the look of confusion Langley wore. He had felt it himself when first confronted by Mary. Logic warred with emotion. "Do not give up too easily," Wes cautioned.

Langley lifted a hand in a wave of acknowledgement as he made his way down the hall.

"He is not a bad fellow," Wes said to Mary as she slipped an arm around his waist. "In fact, he is much better behaved than I ever was..." He looked down at her. "...Until recently, that is."

"Kitty has seemed welcoming whenever she met

him," Mary said. "She even allowed him more than one dance on two occasions."

"And that is significant," Wes teased, earning him a huff.

"It is."

"I do not disagree," he turned and wrapped her in his arms. "He looks like he has lost his heart to her."

"But she says she will not have him."

Wes nodded. "Darcy and Mother will sort it out. All will be well."

"No one outside of our family saw them. They would not have to marry."

Wes shook his head. "Oh, no, my dear. It is far too late for that."

"It is not."

"I saw Langley's face. It is most certainly too late. He can no more walk away from her than I could have walked away from you." He kissed her softly. "I love you Lady Westonbury."

She smiled brilliantly just as he had expected she would.

"And I love you."

And that was a very good thing, for Wes would be lost and wandering in a fog, much like Langley was at present, if Mary did not love him. He had been there, but he was not there any longer.

He lowered his lips to hers and kissed her deeply, longingly, as if she was the very air he needed to breathe, for she was. And as she sighed with contentment, Wes could only wish for his friend to find the same good fortune that had found him. For there was no greater joy than knowing that the woman in his arms and returning his kisses was his and his alone. And tonight, when the last dance had been danced, and the last toast had been made, she would be going home with him, to their house and their bed. His future was just beginning and a gloriously bright one it was and all because he had been granted success in persuading Miss Mary to be his.

Before You Go

If you enjoyed this book, be sure to let others know by leaving a review.

~*~*~

Want to know when other books in this series will be available?

You can always know what's new with my books by subscribing to my mailing list.

(There will, of course, be a thank you gift for joining because I think my readers are awesome!)

Book News from Leenie Brown

(bit.ly/LeenieBBookNews)

~*~*~

Turn the page to read an excerpt of another one of Leenie's books

A Very Mary Christmas Excerpt

If you like stories about Mary Bennet, I have written a few, including A Very Mary Christmas.

Chapter 1

Mary Bennet stood behind her elder sisters, waiting to exit their pew. Her father had already made his escape, but her mother was busy making sure everyone knew that Jane and Elizabeth were soon to be married. Mary watched little flecks of dust dance in the beams of light that streamed through the windows as she listened to her mother. How empty her home would be! How fortunate she was to have daughters so well attached! Mary resisted the urge to roll her eyes and silently tapped an impatient toe inside her boot. Finally, when all the neighbour ladies had heard of her good fortune, Mrs. Bennet moved far enough into the aisle to allow Mary and her sisters to be liberated from their box. Unfortunately, they were not free to leave their mother's side as she shooed them behind her.

"Oh, Mr. Hammond!" Mrs. Bennet's voice rang out through the nave, catching the fine-looking young gentleman before he could escape his pew.

Mary cringed. Must her mother now inform all the gentlemen as well as the ladies? She heaved a resigned sigh as Mr. Hammond turned toward them. Mr. Hammond, you see, was unmarried, nor did he have a sister who would share the joyful news of an upcoming wedding with him. So, Mary realized, her mother, no doubt, thought it her particular duty to tell him. Of course, this was not entirely without benefit, since her mother's need for attention would give Mary a moment or two of admiring him, and for that, she could, perhaps, be grateful.

"Have you heard the news?" Mrs. Bennet continued even before they had reached the place where Mr. Hammond stood. "My two eldest daughters are to be married. The announcement was made at Mr. Bingley's ball, but I do not recall seeing you there." There was a bit of a teasing scold in her tone.

Mr. Nicholas Hammond stretched his lips into a thin smile. Mrs. Bennet had probably wished for him to dance with her daughters. She was always putting forward one or another of them. "I was not in attendance as there were things which required my attention on my estate." A rather lengthy receipt had arrived earlier that day from his father, and Nicholas had been more eager to see his finances settled than he was to dance away the night in a set of clothes that, if his father continued his ways, Nicholas would not be able to afford and keep to his plans.

"Oh, yes, running an estate is such dreadfully taxing work, I am sure."

Mr. Hammond struggled to keep the smile on his face. Mrs. Bennet's voice was grating, and her tone was patronizing.

"There were no banns read," she continued in her same annoying volume of speaking — somewhere between an exclamation and a screech if you asked Nicholas.

"They are to be married by special license. That is why Mr. Darcy and Mr. Bingley are gone to town, you see — to get the license. It is a very proper thing, too, considering their consequence."

Nicholas nodded and attempted to step away, but she stepped forward for every step he took backward. He had little interest in which daughter was marrying which gentleman or when the gentlemen were to be returning or any of the particulars about the double wedding and the breakfast. No, he stopped his failing retreat, that was not entirely true. "They will be returning within the week?" He was nearly certain that was what Mrs. Bennet had said, and he was pleased when she acknowledged it to be true.

"There is a small estate matter I wished to discuss with Mr. Bingley." Typically, he would not have explained such a query, but he knew Mrs. Bennet. She was not unlike a dog intent upon winning a bone and would not cease her inquiries until she had a morsel of information. So, it was best if he provided that morsel himself, rather than leaving it to the imagination of Mrs. Bennet and her friends. He just needed to make sure he told her only as much as he wished broadcast throughout Meryton.

"My Kitty is in good looks today, is she not?"

Ah, there it was. Miss Kitty was to be the one to be promoted now that her eldest sisters were engaged.

The cheeks of the pretty young lady, who stood beside her mother, flushed, and she coughed nervously as her mother prodded her forward while her younger sister did a poor job of catching a giggle behind her hand.

"I had not noticed," Nicholas replied to quell the mother's advances and then, to spare at least some of Miss Kitty's feelings, added, "although I would have to agree now that you have mentioned it." He looked at the rest of the Bennet daughters, who stood behind their mother wearing varying expressions of unease — and who could blame them! They were sensible ladies, unlike their mother and younger sisters. "I believe all of the Bennet ladies are looking fine today."

Nicholas' eyes rested for a moment on Miss Mary. Why was she not the one being thrown forward? She was the next eldest and nearly as pretty as the others. In fact, if he were to be truthful with himself, she was the one he preferred. With this slightly troubling thought in mind, he turned to go, but remembering the beginning of Mrs. Ben-

net's comments and why any of the younger Bennet girls were being promoted, he turned back and
offered his congratulations to Miss Bennet and
Miss Elizabeth. Then, with a shallow bow, he took
his leave.

However, he was only a few steps from the group
when Mrs. Bennet's shrill call to Mrs. Long caused
him to flinch and falter in his steps.

"I must speak to Mrs. Long about the wedding
breakfast preparations." He could hear the excitement in Mrs. Bennet's voice. "Jane, Lizzy, you will
attend me. Mary, go tell your father that I will be
just a few more minutes." There was no mistaking
the commanding tone of the directions, and
Nicholas was just beginning to chuckle to himself
about how wise Mr. Bennet had been to slip out so
quickly at the end of the service when Mrs. Bennet's next comments drove any merriment from his
mind.

"It is what she was born for, I am afraid."

There was a clucking from someone else.
Nicholas assumed without looking back that it
was Mrs. Long. His feet seemed rooted to the floor,
held in place by the shockingly crass comments of
Miss Mary's mother.

"Mama!"

That was probably Miss Bennet, he thought. Her voice was gentler than Miss Elizabeth's.

"She lost her chance when she did not go to town," Mrs. Bennet continued. "Mr. Collins is all but married now."

Ah, yes, Nicholas had heard the Bennet heir was to marry elsewhere, and Mrs. Bennet was none-too-pleased. There was very little hope of being ignorant of your neighbour's business in Meryton, unless you stayed to your house and never ventured out. Even then, the tales might be brought to you by a servant who had heard it from a stable boy who had heard it from the butcher who had indubitably heard it from Mrs. Bennet, Mrs. Long, or one of their friends.

There was more clucking and a sigh from Mrs. Long.

"Now she will be nothing more than a companion or governess. It is best if she begins acting the part."

There was a sad agreement from Mrs. Long and a bit more chiding from one or both of the elder daughters, but Nicholas did not bother to listen. His feet had once again fallen under his command,

and he took two long strides toward the door. "Miss Mary," he called.

Mary stopped her hurried escape from the church. Nicholas could see the embarrassment she felt clearly painted on her cheeks as she turned toward him. It was a feeling with which Nicholas was familiar. His father was no saint.

"Mr. Hammond," Mary greeted, keeping her eyes lowered.

"Do you know on which day, in particular, Mr. Bingley might return?" It was not actually information that he truly needed to know, but it would suffice as an excuse to keep the biddies and their wagging tongues at bay. It would not be the first time that he and Miss Mary had conducted a conversation. They were friends and had on occasion conversed on the street in meeting or most often at an assembly when both he and she had chosen to sit out rather than dance. It was not that he did not like dancing — he did, to a point. Nor was it because Miss Mary lack ability at dancing — she did not. It was the lack of meaningful conversation to be had during a dance that he found annoying. Small talk, the weather, and news of his neighbors were not subjects that interested either to him or

Miss Mary, and, to be honest, this was what he enjoyed most about Miss Mary Bennet — her ability to converse on topics considered non-traditional for a young lady.

He glanced over his shoulder surreptitiously. Seeing that he had caught her mother's attention, he extended an arm to Mary. If her mother wished to promote a lady of quality to any gentleman — and himself, in particular — she should be pushing Miss Mary forward. Miss Kitty and Miss Lydia, though quite pretty, were still too young and foolish to be considered as wives. His arm hung in the air between them while Mary looked at it in confusion. Surely, she knew what he was asking without him saying it, did she not? "Your mother," he said softly.

Mary's eyes widened slightly, and she nodded her understanding before placing her hand lightly on his arm. "I am not her favourite," she replied in a tone equally as soft as his had been. "This may actually lower me in her eyes since she will consider it snatching your attention away from Kitty, but I thank you for the attempt."

Silently, he cursed himself for not considering that. "My apologies," he whispered.

She shook her head and replied quietly. "It is not your fault she is as she is." Then, raising the volume of her voice, she answered his original question. "According to Jane, Mr. Bingley hopes to return to Netherfield by Thursday." She tipped her head and looked up at him. Oh, she did love the auburn tinge to his hair. She flicked her eyes away as his green ones turned towards her. "Are you still thinking of leasing a field?"

"I am." So she remembered their conversation from the last time they had met on the street in Meryton. She was fetching something — he wished he could remember what it was — for her mother, and he had been intent on seeing if Mr. Wilton had a particular book in his shop. "Rose-moore has done exceptionally well this year, and with a bit of the profit, I would like to attempt to increase my holdings and my income."

"It seems a reasonable plan." But when was Nicholas Hammond unreasonable? In her opinion, he was the most level-headed, business-minded man in all of Hertfordshire.

"My father's bills have not decreased," he explained. Again, he knew there was no need to explain himself, but with Mary, he felt at ease and knew he would have an ally. And there was also the hope that she might be of use to him in explaining his need for the land to her soon-to-be-brother.

"Is your mother well?"

It was a very proper question but more than not just a pleasantry for there was a tone of sincere compassion her voice. He smiled. It was just like Mary — proper, yet not indifferent. "She is. It was merely a trifling cough which only kept her from society for a se'ennight, and, according to her most recent letter, now that she is fully recovered, it is a rare afternoon or evening that is not filled with some sort of entertainment and friends. In fact, her schedule was so busy last month that it required a new hat to be purchased since hers had all been worn so many times."

He loved his mother and knew that she was not frivolous or extravagant like his father was. In truth, Nicholas suspected, that it was not his mother who required the hat at all, but rather his father who required it of her. He knew his father had an image he wished to portray, and she, being his wife, must assist him.

As if she knew what he was thinking, Mary smiled sadly at him as she inquired after his brother — his thoughtless, devil-may-care younger brother, Alfred.

"Fred has not been sent up, nor have I received any particularly concerning letters, and since the term will be ending soon, I think he will survive it."

They stood outside the church just slightly apart from the other parishioners who had remained to converse rather than scurrying away since the day was bright and warm for early December.

Mary withdrew her hand from Nicholas' arm and fidgeted with her gloves, making sure they were firmly on each finger. "Will your brother be returning to Rosemoore for his holidays?"

Mr. Hammond sighed and shook his head. "I expect more bills from Bath in the new year. Hertfordshire is too dull for Fred's liking, so he has elected to spend his break with our parents."

"You will not join them in Bath?"

There was again a note of concern in her inquiry. She was not ferreting out information. Nicholas knew her well enough to know that Miss Mary did not tell tales or speak anything less than the truth. He would not be going to Bath. He could not find it in his heart, even for his mother's sake, to spend the money on such a trip, knowing it would be a venture in futility and frustration. He did not say this, however. He just simply shook his head.

Mary understood and did not question further. Sometimes, no matter how much you might wish to love your relations, they made it difficult.

"I wish I could go to Bath." Mary had risen on her toes and was looking, he suspected, for her father.

"I beg your pardon?" he said somewhat surprised by her comment. Mary had never struck him as someone who might wish to travel away from the small village of Meryton. She seemed so at ease here. She walked to town regularly and rambled through the fields as if they were made just for her presence.

Her cheeks, which had just recovered from her previous embarrassment, flushed once again. She had not intended to say that aloud. "Not Bath in particular, just somewhere other than here."

Ah, he understood the comment now. He had felt the same way when he was younger. School had been his escape. "Your mother?" he asked gently.

Mary nodded as her heart raced. Except for Jane

and Elizabeth, she did not speak of her unhappiness to others — especially if that other was a gentleman she wished to notice her for reasons other than her lack of acceptance by her own family. "And my sisters. Oh, not Jane and Lizzy. Kitty and Lydia, and actually, not Kitty, she can be quite nice, but Lydia..." Her voice trailed off as she realized she was babbling. "Oh, there is my father. I must give him my message, or..."

Mr. Hammond held up a hand to stop her and waved her on her way, earning him a grateful smile before she hurried off toward her father.

Glancing back over her shoulder to take one more look at Mr. Hammond, Mary saw that he was still watching her. If only he were watching her for the reasons she wished he would, but he was not. To him, she was a friend, and he was merely concerned for her welfare. She sighed. If only he would see her as more. But, she was plain and read too much and had little to entice a gentleman — her mother's words echoed in her mind. She may have very well lost her chance of having a family of her own by not walking to Meryton last week and pursuing Mr. Collins as her mother suggested. She shuddered at the thought. No, if that were her only hope for marriage, she would gladly accept spinsterhood.

"Papa," she said, tapping his elbow. "Mama is speaking with Mrs. Long and will be a few minutes longer."

Mr. Bennet smiled at her and then placed an arm around her shoulder. "You are a good girl, Mary."

"Thank you, Papa."

He squeezed her shoulder and then removed his arm. "Are you going to wait with me?"

"I would like to walk home." She bit her lip and twisted her fingers together as she waited for his permission.

His smile was understanding. "Is she still upset about Collins?"

Mary smiled at the way her father's lips curled in disgust as he said the name. "She is, and I should like a few moments of solitude."

He chuckled. "It seems your mother has that effect on many — myself included," he added with a wink. "Go on. We will follow shortly, and I will try to work on her again."

"Thank you, Papa." Mary knew that her father would do as he said, but it would be of little use.

Her mother, once set on a notion, was rather immovable.

Mary swung her reticule at her side, letting it brush against the fabric of her pelisse and bang lightly off her leg as she walked. Thoughts of her mother and her future tumbled over each other in her mind. Having reached the spot in the road where she could first see Longbourn, she stopped and considered it for several minutes — the gardens and fields that surrounded the large house with its welcoming drive, the stables and outbuildings, the stand of trees under which she had found refuge on particularly warm summer days... She shook her head slowly as a realization washed over her. She could not stay here. It had never been a terrible home. It had provided her with plenty of enjoyment and pleasant memories, but what would it hold now? A father, who found her eccentricities amusing; a mother, who would continually remind her that she would never be a wife or mother; and younger sisters, who would inevitably parrot everything that their mother said; while her elder sisters, who attempted to protect her, would be gone. Although the sun still shone, the brightness of the day faded, and she wrapped her arms around her middle. It was a bleak reality, and it was hers.

She trudged on toward home, her feet as heavy as her heart. Perhaps if she was destined to be a spinster, she should take up the mantle now. Aunt Gardener might know of some employment to be had in town, or Lizzy might allow her to come for a period of time to Pemberley. Perhaps in Derbyshire, there might be a gentleman as eager to marry as Mr. Collins, who would not be so unbearable — although she was certain, none would be so perfect as Mr. Hammond.

Acknowledgments

There are many who have had a part in the creation of this story. Some have read and commented on it. Some have proofread for grammatical errors and plot holes. Others have not even read the story and a few, I know, will never read it. However, their encouragement and belief in my ability, as well as their patience when I became cranky or when supper was late or the groceries ran low, was invaluable.

And so, I would like to say *thank you* to Zoe, Rose, Kristine, Ben, and Kyle, as well as my patrons on Patreon and the readers who faithfully read all those Thursday posts on my blog. I feel blessed by your help, support, and understanding.

I have not listed my dear husband in the above group because, to me, he deserves his own special thank you, for, without his somewhat pushy insistence that I start sharing my writing, none of my writing goals and dreams would have been met.

~*~*~

For those who might be interested in some of the visual inspiration I used while writing this book — I have a Pinterest board for that.

Other Leenie B Books

You can find all of Leenie's books at this link
bit.ly/LeenieBBooks
where you can explore the collections below

~*~

Other Pens, Mansfield Park

~*~

Touches of Austen Collection

~*~

Other Pens, Pride and Prejudice

~*~

Dash of Darcy and Companions Collection

~*~

Marrying Elizabeth Series

~*~

Willow Hall Romances

~*~

The Choices Series

~*~

Darcy Family Holidays

~*~

Darcy and... An Austen-Inspired Collection

About the Author

Leenie Brown has always been a girl with an active imagination, which, while growing up, was both an asset, providing many hours of fun as she played out stories, and a liability, when her older sister and aunt would tell her frightening tales. At one time, they had her convinced Dracula lived in the trunk at the end of the bed she slept in when visiting her grandparents!

Although it has been years since she cowered in her bed in her grandparents' basement, she still has an imagination which occasionally runs away with her, and she feeds it now as she did then — by reading!

Her heroes, when growing up, were authors, and the worlds they painted with words were (and still are) her favourite playgrounds! Now, as an adult, she spends much of her time in the Regency world, playing with the characters from her favourite Jane Austen novels and those of her own creation.

When she is not traipsing down a trail in an attempt to keep up with her imagination, Leenie resides in the beautiful province of Nova Scotia with her two sons and her very own Mr. Brown (a wonderful mix of all the best of Darcy, Bingley, and Edmund with a healthy dose of the teasing Mr. Tilney and just a dash of the scolding Mr. Knight-ley).

Connect with Leenie

E-mail:
LeenieBrownAuthor@gmail.com
Facebook:
www.facebook.com/LeenieBrownAuthor
Blog:
leeniebrown.com
Patreon:
https://www.patreon.com/LeenieBrown
Subscribe to Leenie's Mailing List:
Book News from Leenie Brown
(bit.ly/LeenieBBookNews)